T5-CUV-885

A SOUND of CRYING

A SOUND
of CRYING

Rodie Sudbery

SCHOLASTIC BOOK SERVICES
NEW YORK · TORONTO · LONDON · AUCKLAND · SYDNEY · TOKYO

This book is sold subject to the condition that it shall not be resold, lent, or otherwise circulated in any binding or cover other than that in which it is published—unless prior written permission has been obtained from the publisher—and without a similar condition, including this condition, being imposed on the subsequent purchaser.

First published in Great Britain by Andre Deutsch Limited 1968
as THE HOUSE IN THE WOOD

Copyright © 1970 by Rodie Sudbery. This edition is published by Scholastic Book Services, a division of Scholastic Magazines, Inc., by arrangement with The McCall Publishing Company.

1st printing .... February 1972

Printed in the U.S.A.

For My Mother and Father

✦ Contents

A SOUND of CRYING

1 ✦ *The Young Scientist*

Frederick sliced the top off his boiled egg and gazed absently into its depths. He couldn't see the future there, but he didn't need to. He knew well enough that for the next few weeks his peaceful vacation would be completely disrupted.

Why on earth had his aunt fallen ill just now? He didn't want to spend the summer with a gang of infants underfoot. True, Polly was twelve, only a year younger than himself; but she was a girl. Although that hadn't mattered five years ago, he thought it would now.

"Frederick, is there something the matter with that egg?"

He came to life at his mother's voice, stirring the yolk and sniffing. "It seems to smell quite normal. Why, have you cooked me a doubtful one?"

"Don't be silly, of course not. I just wondered why you weren't eating it. You'll miss the bus if you don't hurry."

He glanced at his watch and resignedly started to bolt

the egg. It was better than nothing. His mother and Mrs. Richards had been too busy getting bedrooms ready to cook a real lunch. His cousins should have given more warning of their coming, he thought crossly. And now he was expected to waste an afternoon going in to town to meet their train.

Of course, he had to admit that it wouldn't be entirely wasted. He had run out of hydrochloric acid and ammonia, and had been waiting until his mother wanted some town shopping done; but this was just as good a pretext for getting his fares paid. The newsstand might have the latest *Young Scientist* in as well.

He wondered if he would recognize his cousins. Last time he saw them Michael and Jennifer had been toddlers and the youngest hadn't even been born.

"Have you got a crib for Hugh?" he asked, pushing back his chair.

"Hardly. He's five."

"Good heavens, I suppose he is."

On the bus he worked out that Michael and Jennifer must now be nine and eight respectively. Relieved at having it straight, he opened the book he had brought with him and found his place. It was very interesting, all about crystals, but somehow he found he couldn't concentrate. It wasn't because he was on a bus; he always read on the bus home from school. He stopped trying and let his thoughts wander idly: science lessons at school, talking to Mr. Bates afterwards, the neat red tens on his homework. But then there was the other side of it: the idiots who jeered at him for working so hard and taking it so seriously. He would never "cook" his lab results to make them more satisfactory, and as for fooling around during practical classes, that was unthinkable; he was always too busy. His friends found him hard to understand and his enemies didn't try. Yes, it was really much better during vacations, when he could devote himself exclusively to chemistry. He had planned so many things to do: books to read, experiments to try. And now everything would have to wait.

"Are we nearly there?" asked Jennifer with a yawn.

"Wait a minute," said Michael from his position of concentrated attention by the window. "There's one due . . . yes . . . a hundred and five miles."

"Five miles to go," said Polly. When they had realized that they could read the distance traveled from numbers posted by the tracks, she had discovered from the guard that it was a hundred and ten miles to their destination. After that they had kept an exact watch on the progress of their journey. "Time to get the luggage down." She stood on the seat and reached for the suitcases.

"Five miles is a lot," said Jennifer doubtfully.

"Not on a train," said Polly.

"Really?" Jennifer became excited and jumped up beside her.

"No, I'll get them," said Polly. "You might stumble. You pick up all the candy wrappers and things. We can't leave it looking like this."

They had had an empty compartment, and had rather spread themselves. The journey had been fun. Polly almost wished it didn't have to end. She was excited about seeing Frederick again, but also slightly nervous. She wondered if he remembered his visit to them when he was seven with as much pleasure as she did. She had felt rather guilty at her delight two days ago when their father had told them they were to come here; although he and the doctor had both been assuring them that they needn't worry about their mother, it didn't seem right not to be miserable.

Another train hurtled past the window and Michael flinched back.

"Why are you frightened?" asked Hugh from the opposite seat. "It can't get us in here."

"I'm not, it just makes me jump," said Michael defensively.

"It doesn't make *me* jump."

"Hugh, help with the candy wrappers," ordered Polly.

He crawled obediently around the floor but asked: "Why doesn't Michael help too?"

"It's his turn for the window."

"So was it mine."

"You're too small to watch the mileposts," said Jennifer.

"A hundred and nine!" said Michael, and began to chant in time with the rhythm of the train: "Hundred and nine, hundred and nine, hundred and nine. . . ."

"We're near-ly there, we're near-ly there," Jennifer joined in, cramming a sticky handful of papers into one of the ashtrays. "Hey, we're slowing down! There's the station! We're near-ly there, we're near-ly there, we're . . . near . . . ly . . . there."

Polly kicked some crumbs under the seat "Here, Michael, you carry this, and Jennifer bring the coats."

"What about me?" said Hugh.

"You bring Number Three."

"Suppose Frederick isn't here?" said Michael anxiously as they got out.

"Shall I run up and down looking for him?" suggested Jennifer.

"No, stay with me," said Polly. "You wouldn't recognize him anyway. . . . I think that's him over there."

Frederick spotted a string of unattended children who must be his cousins and went towards them, noticing how untidy they looked. Polly had grown, but her small bony face hadn't changed much.

"Frederick? I almost wouldn't have known you. You didn't used to wear specs. They do make you look different."

Her voice was as he remembered it too, clear and confident.

"I've worn glasses for years," he said rather crossly, and added: "A good thing I knew you."

"Yes. I expect you can guess which is which of these —Michael, Jennifer, Hugh."

He nodded to them. The two older ones were alike, thin and brown-eyed. Hugh had a fringe growing into his eyes and clutched a battered teddy bear; Frederick thought he looked like a poster for an orphanage. The thumb that he removed from his mouth in order to say hello was an oasis of pink on his dirty hand.

Frederick took one of the suitcases and led them out of the station. "I've just got to go to a couple of shops. You can wait for me by the bus stop."

"Oh, we'll come too," said Polly. "I feel like a little walk."

"I'm only going across the road," he said, but found

that they followed him all the same. "There'll be a walk when we get off the bus," he added.

"Good," said Polly.

When he made his purchases Jennifer chirped in astonishment: "Hydrochloric acid!"

"Have you got a chemistry set?" asked Michael.

"Yes," he said shortly.

"Gosh, you *are* lucky," said Polly.

"There you are, young man," said Mr. Bage, handing him the neatly sealed package; and added as usual: "Don't blow yourself up!"

Jennifer giggled, and Frederick concealed his irritation with difficulty.

"Are you interested in chemistry, then?" he asked Polly as they went out.

"Well, I hate learning it, but mixing things together must be fun."

"Can we try it?" asked Michael.

"Experimenting is dangerous without sufficient knowledge," said Frederick, and that seemed to close the subject.

Polly was afraid this remark applied to her as well as to the younger ones. She felt dejected at having said the wrong thing; it seemed all too easy to do with this new, cross Frederick. She wished she had pretended to be a genius at science, but then he would probably have seen through her very quickly. He looked dreadfully clever, what with the glasses and the book he was carrying, whose title she had managed to glimpse: *An Introduction to Crystallography*. She was not surprised when the magazine he bought was called *The Young Scientist*.

"Is that for your father?" asked Jennifer.

"Of course not," rebuked Polly quickly, "it's for himself."

Frederick thought it would have been better if she had told Jennifer to mind her own business. They recrossed the road and Hugh, lagging behind, narrowly escaped being run over.

Nobody talked much on the bus. Polly kept giving Frederick furtive sidelong glances, trying to find an echo of the impish companion he had been five years ago. She wished he would take his glasses off for a moment and let her see if the face she remembered lurked beneath, but she couldn't bring herself to the point of asking him.

The promised walk was down a winding country lane.

"How lonely it is," said Polly with pleasure. "Do you get cut off by the snow in winter?"

"We haven't been yet. I suppose in a bad winter it could happen. It is lonely, though. Our nearest neighbors are half a mile away, that village where we got off the bus."

"So do you keep a stock of canned food in case?"

"Mother might," he said vaguely.

"And candles in case the electricity failed," continued Polly, "and a big pile of logs."

"Why not coal?" he asked dampingly.

"All right then, coal. You'd have to dig a path to the coal shed. Oh, you are lucky; we'll never be snowed in where we live."

Frederick couldn't see that this was a matter for regret.

"I'm sure we've come more than half a mile since we got off the bus," said Jennifer plaintively.

"You see those pine trees at the bend? The gate is there," said Frederick.

"Oh, do you live in a wood?" Jennifer cheered up.

"It's a very small wood," warned Frederick.

"Nice, even so," said Polly, and added half to herself, "If you ran out of coal you could cut down a tree."

Once they were through the gate the wood didn't seem small to her. The trees grew too thickly for her to see how far they stretched, and the winding drive was shadowed and dim. It was very pleasant after the hot, dusty road.

"There's a mysterious kind of smell," she said, sniffing deeply.

Frederick frowned, and sniffed also. "Perfectly ordinary smell of pine trees."

"And of mystery," said Polly. "Lovely." Then they rounded another bend into sunlight and stopped to stare.

Against a background of great pines, the gray stone house stood dark and forbiddingly plain. In front of it the drive widened into a gravel courtyard, and on the far side of this the ground dropped away to a sheet of still water, black with reflections of the trees that hemmed the farther rim. Just where they stood, a little leaf-smothered stream ran under the drive and trickled with scarcely a sound into the lake.

"Oh, what a sinister place to live," breathed Polly. "I bet it's haunted."

Hugh's eyes widened; Michael and Jennifer clasped hands and shrank towards her.

"It most certainly is not," said Frederick, extremely

annoyed. His momentary pride in the scene was shattered.

"How do you know?" asked Jennifer.

"Because there's no such thing as ghosts," he snapped.

"There's one in our attic at home," said Michael.

"Captain," nodded Jennifer.

"He's a little old man with a stick."

"We hear him tapping."

Frederick rubbed his nose, exasperated. He never knew how to talk to young children. He remembered there had been a terrible uproar some years ago when he had told a five-year-old that there was no Santa Claus. But surely Michael, at least, was too old for this kind of nonsense.

"Who told you about him?" he asked finally.

"Never mind Captain now," said Polly hastily, but too late; Michael had already replied, "Polly did." It was her turn to feel cross. Things like Captain were spoilt if told to the kind of person Frederick had become.

The front door opened, and a voice called: "Frederick, why don't you bring your cousins inside?"

Polly's vague pleasant memory of an aunt like a storybook queen vanished when she saw Aunt Sylvia. She was alarmingly elegant, and her face looked "arranged" thought Polly, must take ages; and she compared it with her mother's kind tired one which already had wrinkles.

"Hello, Aunty," she said, dumping her suitcase on the hall floor and expecting to be kissed. Instead there was a tinkling musical-box laugh.

"Oh dear, I don't think I can be an aunty, I don't feel

a bit like one. You children had better call me Aunt Sylvia. Now let me look at you all. Dear dear, it must have been a tiring journey; Frederick will show you upstairs and you'll want to tidy up and wash before supper."

Polly supposed they did look rather scruffy, though it hadn't occurred to her before. She felt slightly downcast, but cheered up when she saw her room. It was on the second floor, right up under the eaves with its own narrow flight of stairs.

"A garret!" she said, but seeing Frederick's expression amended: "A very luxurious garret." Frederick, unsmiling, pushed his glasses farther up his nose and clacked away down the stairs. Polly sat on her bed and sighed. He wasn't a bit nice any more. Probably they were going to have a horrible time here. Then she looked round her; it was really very garrety if you concentrated on the sloping ceiling and dormer window and ignored things like the bedside rug and dressing table, and she felt, as when she had first seen the house, a tingling thrill of excitement.

When Uncle Clement came home he shook each of their hands vigorously and hoped they would enjoy their visit. "Frederick will do his best to entertain you, but you musn't expect too much of him," he said with a smile to Polly, who felt like replying that she had already realized that. "He's not very used to girls."

The three younger ones were in bed early. Michael and Jennifer voiced their indignation privately to Polly.

"Why should you stay up later?"

"Because I'm older."

"It's not our bedtime yet. We won't be able to go to sleep."

"You can read for a bit."

"We'd rather you told us a story."

"Yes, well I can't, because I shall be busy downstairs."

"Hey," hissed Michael suddenly, "was Frederick always like this?"

"You told us he was nice," accused Jennifer.

"He's changed," said Polly glumly.

"I don't like him," said Jennifer.

Downstairs Polly found Frederick reading his magazine and felt awed and irritated. Could he really like that kind of thing?

"There's an interesting article here, Dad," he said, and continued in some detail. After a while Aunt Sylvia broke in.

"You must get your hair cut soon, Frederick, and you might as well take Hugh with you." She flashed a smile at Polly. "I don't suppose your mother's been up to seeing to that kind of thing lately."

"I suppose not," said Polly, thinking that Hugh's opinion about a haircut, or at any rate hers, could at least have been asked first.

"On my own?" asked Frederick rather blankly.

"Polly can go with you. You can show her around; it will make a nice little trip for both of you."

"Around what?" muttered Frederick to himself.

"I would like to have a look at that article, if I may," said his father, and he felt pleased.

"Do you believe in ghosts, Dad?" he asked suddenly. Polly looked up.

Uncle Clement smiled. "Which ghosts?"

"Well—just ghosts," said Frederick, nonplussed.

"You don't have a particular one in mind?"

A small hiccup of laughter escaped Polly.

"How could I when they don't exist?"

"You've made up your mind already, have you?"

"Well—do they?" Frederick was very pink and Polly began to feel a little sorry for him.

"It's a difficult question, son," said his father kindly. "I can't say I believe in any ghost I've ever heard of— that's to say, I wouldn't be afraid to go inside Borley Rectory or any of the other famous haunts—but there is certainly quite a weight of evidence in favor of the existence of psychic phenomena."

Polly got left behind here. When she had succeeded in unraveling his meaning to herself she sat feeling smugly victorious and not looking at Frederick, who said no more.

2 ♠ *The Pool*

In the morning Polly was awakened by Michael and Jennifer.

"Go away," she growled. "You're interrupting my dream."

"Oh, please wake up, Polly," said Michael.

She opened her eyes and yawned. "It feels terribly early. You're dressed."

"It's sunny outside," said Jennifer.

"If you get up we can go and explore on our own without Frederick," wheedled Michael.

Polly, wriggling her toes, admitted to herself that this was an attractive plan. "All right," she said.

Ten minutes later she unbolted the back door and let them out into the garden. It gave way to woodland at the top of a long sloping lawn.

"The grass is all wet," said Michael.

"Dew." Polly looked dubiously at their sandaled feet. "Try to walk carefully."

They had damp ankles when they reached the trees.

Here the ground was hummocky and dappled with sunlight, and grass grew in tufts, fine and silky like tender green hair.

"It's cushion grass," said Jennifer, sitting on it. "All soft."

In the hollows behind the tufts were pine needles, and here and there were scattered little black marbles.

"Rabbit droppings," said Polly.

"Oh, I want to see a rabbit," said Jennifer.

"I doubt that you will. They keep out of the way."

"Listen," said Michael, and they all heard a faint murmuring thread of sound. He ran on ahead. "It's a stream," he called.

"It must be the one that goes under the drive," said Polly. "It's nicer up here."

The water slid and racketed on its way, perfectly clear, although there were numerous small obstructions in its course where dead leaves piled up against twigs and stones. Polly found a stick and knocked one out of the way.

"You've made it run all dirty," said Jennifer disapprovingly.

Polly used her stick to walk with instead, and they began to go up through the wood, clambering over rocks and around bushes, lured on by the stream. It ran now louder, now softer, glinting in the leafy sunshine. Invisible birds twittered overhead.

Presently other sounds were drowned by a soft approaching roar.

"What are we coming to?" wondered Michael.

"Oh, look!" said Polly, pointing. It was a splendid

waterfall, quite two feet high, with a flurry of foam at its foot.

"Real spray," said Jennifer, holding her hand out.

Above the fall the water collected behind the careful dam of boulders to form a long clear pool.

"We could paddle," said Michael.

"No," said Polly in hushed tones. "It's deeper than it looks. It would come over your knees."

"It's beautiful," murmured Jennifer.

"Yes . . . why are we whispering?" whispered Michael.

"So we are. I don't know," whispered Polly; and they continued to do so.

"Do you think Frederick made it?"

"No, it's older than that. Look at the moss on the stones. It's been here a long time."

The bed of the pool showed tawny through the reflections of trees and sky. The trees stood round, tall and silent. Polly looked down the slope.

"You can't see the house."

Then she looked the other way, and just a little farther on was a high stone wall, gray-green with lichen, with the stream tumbling out through a hole at its foot. The unexpected sight of something so large and solid made her jump.

"What?" gasped Michael.

Did she catch his uneasiness, or had he already caught hers? "Why does this place feel frightening?" she whispered slowly. "Is there something here?"

"Oh don't," begged Michael, grabbing for her hand.

"What?" said Jennifer loudly, looking from one to the other. "What is it?"

"Shut up," hissed Polly, frozen; the air seemed to reverberate with the echoes of Jennifer's voice. But she refused to shut up.

"I don't like it!" she wailed.

Something snapped inside Polly, and unreasoning terror took hold of her.

"Let's go," she said urgently, and at once they fled, leaping over obstacles and ducking under branches. In a fraction of the time it had taken them to ascend the slope they were back on the lawn. Panting, shuddering, hair and shoes full of twiggy fragments, they stood and gazed at each other.

"What *was* it?" said Jennifer. "There wasn't anything there, was there?"

"I thought Polly saw something," said Michael.

"Only a wall," said Polly. "It wasn't that. It was the pool that was frightening."

"I felt as though something was chasing us," he said.

"No," said Polly definitely. "It was the place, and a place can't chase you. We're all right now."

"I don't understand," complained Jennifer.

"Neither do I. It's a mystery. But it was an adventure, wasn't it?" said Polly in lighter tones.

"Yes," they replied doubtfully.

They went indoors and surprised Uncle Clement, who was making coffee in the kitchen.

"Early risers, hmm? I'm afraid breakfast won't be ready yet for a while. What do you think of the grounds?"

"It must be nice to have a wood of your own," said Polly.

"Yes and no, yes and no. Pleasant for youngsters, of course. Perhaps Frederick will discover some of its charm with your assistance.

Polly wondered what she ought to reply to this, and in the end said nothing. She accepted a cup of coffee, and the other two had orange juice. Frederick was the next down. He commented on their wet feet.

"Have you been playing in the lake?" asked Uncle Clement.

"No," said Polly.

"I'd rather you didn't, unless you can swim. How many of you can? Just Polly; I see. Where have you been then?"

"Up by the stream."

"Did you get as far as the little pool? Pretty, isn't it?"

"Yes," said Polly grudgingly. "It's rather eerie."

Uncle Clement laughed indulgently. Polly asked if he knew who had made it, but he didn't; it had been there when he bought the house. Then he said they had better go and change into dry socks.

"Why didn't you tell them what happened?" asked Jennifer, upstairs.

"I thought Frederick would laugh," said Polly, and to herself she wondered: What did happen?

Aunt Sylvia decreed that the visit to the barber's must take place that day. Michael and Jennifer stayed behind.

"You can't bring that bear," said Frederick disapprovingly.

"His fur needs cutting, doesn't it, Polly?" protested Hugh.

"I don't think they'll do it for you here, Hugh. Number Three can wait until next time. The man at home snips a bit off for him," Polly explained.

"It'll soon be bald at that rate," said Frederick.

"Number Three's fur grows," stated Hugh.

"It does seem to," said Polly.

"How could it possibly? You just forget how long it was to start with."

Polly knew this was probably true, but Frederick didn't have to say so. Hugh liked to think it grew, and in a babyish way so did she.

"Why do you call it Number Three?"

"That's his name," said Polly. "He was mine once." Frederick thought she must be sulking, but in fact she couldn't see that a fuller answer was required. Hugh did bring the bear, but agreed to leave it with Polly while they were in the barber's. She walked up and down the main street with it, looking at the shops and studying the menu in the window of a café. Then she rejoined Frederick and an altered Hugh.

"What a neat little head!" she said, and ruffled it, to Frederick's disapproval.

"Do you want to do anything before we get the bus home? We've got half an hour," he said.

"Let's go and eat sundaes," suggested Polly.

"I haven't any money for that kind of thing."

Polly felt sorry for him. "I'll pay," she said, and Frederick wavered, swayed by his appetite. "I've got a lot of vacation money."

"Well, thank you," said Frederick awkwardly.

At the school he was the only boy who never ate candy. He saved all his pocket money, and would soon have enough for a microscope.

"What's your favorite subject at school?" he asked Polly.

"English. I suppose yours is science. Are you going to be a scientist when you grow up?"

"I want to do chemical research."

"Do you get all A's in chemistry?"

"Usually," he said modestly. Actually he always did. "Do you in English?"

Polly made a face. "No. I don't like grammar."

Frederick laid down his spoon and then felt in his pocket. "I think I can pay for these after all," he discovered. "I've got the change from the bus fare and barber money. I'm sure Mother won't mind."

Polly noted an unexpected point in Aunt Sylvia's favor.

"Do you remember the day you ate six ice creams?" he asked suddenly.

"Yes. I was sick in the gutter."

"Neapolitan sick, because that was the kind of ice cream it was."

"It was your fault. You bet me I couldn't eat six."

They grinned at each other. "We had fun that vacation," said Polly.

"We were very little," said Frederick, solemn again. Life must be grim for him, thought Polly. Nothing but chemistry.

That night she dreamed. She was walking down the drive for the first time again, but she was a different person. She was dressed all in black; her mother had just died, and she was coming to live with her uncle. She was miserable and cold, and she carried a small suitcase.

Now she came to the house. How large it was! The front door looked very impressive, but before she could look for another she heard loud barking and an Alsatian bounded into view. He checked when he saw her, then came slowly on, uttering deep-throated growls. She ran for the steps and banged on the knocker, terrified.

She was pressing against the door and when it opened she fell into the arms of her rescuer. He set her upright, frowning; he was tall and black-bearded.

"Sarah Gray? This is a strange manner of arrival."

"I'm sorry," she stammered. "The dog—"

"Frightened of the beast?" He sounded contemptuous. "Here, Thugdon! Good boy. Back to your kennel now." The dog ran away, wagging its tail. "You had nothing to fear. Thugdon wouldn't harm anyone unless I told him to do so. Come now, let me shut the door. Don't use this entrance again."

"No, Uncle."

"What, what?" He spoke sharply. "Did you say Uncle?"

"I'm sorry—I thought you must be my Uncle Simon —"

He frowned. "I'd rather you didn't call me that. I may as well tell you I don't feel disposed to consider you a relation. My parents closed their doors to your mother when she broke their hearts by running away with a penniless fool; she was no sister of mine after that."

Sarah said nothing. She felt lost and confused.

"There's bad blood in you," he muttered somberly.

"No there isn't," cried Sarah, scarlet, tears springing to her eyes.

He raised his gaze to her face. "Are you contradicting me? I don't advise it, in your position. You have no claim on me, you know. I take you in purely as a charity."

"I am grateful," said Sarah quietly.

"I would prefer your calling me sir."

"Very well, sir."

"I will show you your room. Come with me."

She followed him up two flights of stairs to a little white attic. "Did my mother sleep here?"

"Don't be foolish, girl. This was a servants' room when my parents were alive. Now that I am alone I don't need servants; a woman comes in from the village each day." He turned to go, then paused. "And, Sarah, you will oblige me by not mentioning your mother. Do you understand?"

"Yes, sir."

"You may unpack your luggage now."

He went away. She opened her suitcase, but all she took out was a shawl that had been her mother's. It was faded, but the colors were still pretty. She wrapped it round her (the room was cold) and sat on the bed. Tears poured down her cheeks. "Mother," she whispered. "Mother."

Presently she roused herself and went on with her unpacking. The suitcase contained everything she owned; a small number of shabby personal possessions, including some things that had been her mother's.

Everything larger had been sold to pay for her mother's funeral. When she had finished she spread the shawl on her bed to cover as much as possible of the coarse brown blanket.

Later, while they ate a cold supper, her uncle said: "I received a letter from some woman by the name of Pigwash, or Pigswill—"

"Miss Swirles, sir?" suggested Sarah, naming the teacher of the little school she had attended.

"There is no need to interrupt. I was about to say that I gather your brains are unlikely to earn you a living . . ." (Sarah knew she was not good at lessons, but Miss Swirles had always been very patient with her, and she wondered if she had really put it so unkindly) ". . . and you are not trained to any skill. I have therefore asked Mrs. Piper to instruct you in the art of housework, and we must hope you will be able to go into service at some big house, since I can't afford to keep you idle forever."

"No, sir," murmured Sarah, when he paused as though for an answer.

"Is that all you have to say, girl?"

"I—I'll work hard, sir."

"See that you do."

Sarah was too numb with misery to feel more than a dull interest in her fate. She didn't think her mother would have liked her to be a servant, but already she felt it would be preferable to living here with her uncle.

"Shall I wash these things, sir?" she said when they had finished their meal.

"Certainly not. I don't want my good china broken by an ignorant girl. You may put them carefully on to the trolley and wheel it into the kitchen for Mrs. Piper."

She wondered whether to tell him that she had done the dishes for her mother for as long as she could remember, but didn't dare.

"Give those scraps to Thugdon, and see if he needs a drink. His kennel is outside the back door."

She carried the plate of scraps outside and, peering around in the dusk, located the kennel a few yards away. She began to creep towards it. At once there was a shifting sound and the dog's head poked out. She stood still.

"Good boy," she said timidly. Thugdon watched her in silence, and after a moment she went forward again. She could see two bowls right under his nose. Must she really go that close? Wouldn't he eat the scraps off the ground if she left them here? But she had to see if he needed a drink.

Both bowls were empty. He stood quite still while she scraped the plate into one; but when she tried to pick up the other he gave a terrible growl. She jumped back, stood undecided for a moment, and then returned miserably to the kitchen. Her uncle was waiting for her; he had a little smile on his lips, but this vanished almost at once.

"How dare you take that plate out of the house?" he barked.

"It—it had the scraps on—sir," faltered Sarah.

"What do you suppose your fingers are for? Eh? You can't afford fastidious ways now, you know."

"I'm sorry, sir."

"Didn't he need a drink?"

"Yes, sir, but—he wouldn't let me take his bowl."

There was a small silence. "Go and get it," he commanded coldly.

Sarah turned slowly to the door.

"Hurry!"

Thugdon was just finishing the scraps. "Good boy," pleaded Sarah. "Good Thugdon. Let me take your bowl and fetch you some water. . . ." She stretched her hand out slowly. He began to growl. She grasped the bowl, and he put a paw on it from the other side. She began to sweat with fright, but made herself keep still. "Please let me have it, Thugdon." She pulled at it gently. He suddenly lifted his paw and gave a short sharp bark. It sounded almost like a laugh.

When she took the bowl into the kitchen her uncle said: "I told you to hurry."

"I was as quick as I could be, sir," she replied quietly.

"Sarah." His voice was even quieter than hers. "Don't let me have to warn you too often about impertinence. My patience is not inexhaustible."

As he left her the kitchen dissolved into a sunlit bedroom, at which Polly, still half in the dream, looked with amazement.

3 ✤ *Polly Begins a Story*

Gradually her head cleared. What an odd dream it had been! Almost a nightmare. She lay recalling its details; they were all quite clear in her memory. The way this room had looked, for instance, with bare boards and no furniture except a black iron bedstead and a scrubbed wooden chest-of-drawers. And the appearance of Sarah's uncle, with his black beard and his dreary old-fashioned clothes. Her dreams had never been set in the past before.

"That poor girl," she said aloud; "I am glad I'm not her really." And for a moment Sarah's grief for her mother was real and poignant again inside her, leaving her very cold. Mother, she thought in a panic, what if Mother dies?

"I expect Mother will be better soon," she remarked casually at breakfast to nobody in particular.

"I'm sure she will," said Uncle Clement. "After a good rest she'll be a different person."

"I want her to be the *same* person," growled Hugh.

After breakfast Aunt Sylvia asked Polly and Frederick to do the dishes. Polly looked around the kitchen with new interest. In her dream the gas stove hadn't been there; just the old-fashioned built-in range.

"Do you ever cook on that?" she asked, pointing to it.

"Heavens no," said Frederick. "Sometimes we light the fire in winter, but that's all. It warms the kitchen, and the cat likes to sit in the top oven."

"It's an unsightly thing," said Aunt Sylvia, passing through. "I should have it removed."

"I like it," protested Polly.

"You would," said Frederick.

"Was my room a maids' room once?" Polly asked.

"What odd things you say!" said her aunt with a vexed little laugh. "I suppose it may have been in the past."

"It's a very nice room," added Polly politely.

Aunt Sylvia looked at the rain which was falling steadily outside. "Such a nuisance, this weather. I hope you children can find something to occupy you indoors today. Frederick, what can you suggest?"

He hunched himself over the pan he was scouring and didn't reply.

"Aren't there some card games somewhere?"

Polly felt that Aunt Sylvia was being mean to him. "I know," she exclaimed, "you could do an experiment for us."

"Be careful then, won't you, Frederick," said his mother, and went out again.

"Oh please do, I should so love to watch one," begged

Polly. "Only the seniors are allowed in the lab at school."

"I have to make my bed first."

"We'll do ours at the same time."

Frederick's room impressed them all with its array of test-tubes and neatly labeled bottles.

"NaCl; KMnO$_4$; dilute HCl; dilute H$_2$SO$_4$," read Polly.

"What's dilute? It's on lots of them," said Jennifer.

"It means diluted," said Frederick patiently. "Chemists can't sell children concentrated acids. Lots of things are difficult to get; the dentist gave me my mercury."

"The dentist?"

"They use it in fillings. Quicksilver is another name for it." He showed it to them and they passed it round, exclaiming with delight at its heaviness, and the way it didn't wet the sides of the bottle. Frederick began to enjoy himself.

"Watch," he said, dropping a pinch of white powder into a beaker of water and stirring it up; the water turned a pretty blue.

"Is it magic?" asked Hugh.

"Anhydrous copper sulphate becoming hydrated," he replied, and left Hugh certain that it was indeed magic.

"Potassium permanganate," he said, putting dark crystals into another beaker and slowly adding water. Then he heated the beaker over a bunsen burner and beautiful streams of purple color curled hither and thither in the water. "Convection currents."

"Make an explosion," suggested Polly.

He prepared a test-tube of hydrogen and held a lighted match outside it. The flame was sucked into the tube with a squeaky pop.

"That wasn't very loud," said Jennifer.

Right, thought Frederick. Reaching into a cupboard, he found an empty can with holes punched into the bottom and lid. "This will be a bit louder," he murmured, placing the can with the bottom hole just over the bunsen burner and switching the gas on. "First we fill the can with gas." He switched off and placed the can on a tripod. "Then we light the gas." He applied a match to the hole in the lid and made the can look like a large, eccentric night light. His audience watched, fascinated. "The gas gets used up as the flame burns . . . until eventually . . ." he paused, and something in his expression made Polly feel nervous ". . . the flame goes *inside the can* to find out what's happening . . ." The flame vanished, and with a colossal bang the lid of the can blew off and hit the ceiling.

"Frederick, you fiend!" said Polly. Michael and Jennifer had been rendered speechless.

"Number Three doesn't like bangs," remarked Hugh; and went out, cradling the bear against his shoulder.

Frederick retrieved the lid of his can and said he would prepare oxygen next. The two younger ones became bored while this was going on and were discovered at the end of the experiment playing with bobbles of mercury on the window sill.

"That's *very* naughty!" said Frederick angrily. "You'll get it dirty, and it's very difficult to clean. And you've probably lost some. And also it's extremely poisonous." He coaxed the drops into one and slid it back into the bottle.

"Mercury poisoning makes your mouth go all green . . . and you smell *terrible*," said Polly dreamily.

"How do you know?" Frederick didn't believe it.

"I once overheard two women talking on a bus."

"Just the kind of thing you would overhear." He said it quite nicely, and Polly decided not to feel insulted.

Next he mixed metal filings with some pale yellow powder.

"Is that sherbet?" asked Michael hopefully.

"No, sulphur," said Frederick, heating the mixture.

"It's gone all black and nasty," said Jennifer.

Frederick removed it from the heat and poured a little acid on top. A terrible smell filled the room.

"*Pooh!*" gasped Michael. "Bad eggs!"

"I'm choking," exclaimed Jennifer; and the two of them decided they'd had enough of chemistry.

"Hydrogen sulphide," said Frederick smugly, closing the door behind them and opening the window. Polly went and hung out while he fanned the air busily.

"You did that to get rid of them," she accused suddenly.

Frederick grinned. "It worked, didn't it?"

"You're a cunning old magician." A thought struck her. "Did you want to get rid of me, too?"

"No," said Frederick truthfully. "I don't mind you."

"Let's make a poisonous gas. Can we?

"Carbon dioxide."

"Isn't there something more poisonous than that?"

"Sulphur dioxide—we could make that."

"Oh good, and since the others have gone I could have a little sniff of it, couldn't I?"

"I think it would be better if you didn't. Why do you want to?"

"Oh, it would be such fun. Please, just a little sniff."

When he had made the gas he relented, and feeling he mustn't be outdone by Polly he had a sniff, too. It made their eyes run and caught at the backs of their throats.

"Like matches," said Polly.

"Exactly."

"What are you going to do with the rest of it?"

"Put it out of the window. I think we'd better clean up now."

"Are you ever called anything for short? Frederick is such a mouthful." Polly began to help.

"They sometimes call me Fred at school. I hate it."

"Fred." Polly giggled. "Yes, it doesn't really suit you. What did I call you when we were little?"

"Something silly, I expect." He scraped at the remains of the hydrogen sulphide experiment. Thinking about being called Fred had made him morose. But Polly looked so downcast that he summoned up a small grin to soften his remark.

"Something like Duff," she was encouraged to muse. "No, I know. Fluff. Because your hair was."

"Well, it isn't now." He passed a hand over his smooth head. "And if you're going to call me that, please don't do it when anyone else can hear."

"All right, Fluff," said Polly meekly.

When they had put everything away she went up to her room to write letters home.

"Is Mother getting better?" she asked her father. "I dreamed she was dead, it was horrid." After a moment she added "But it wasn't her, really."

A floorboard creaked behind her, and she put her hand quickly over what she had written before she turned round. But nobody was reading the letter over her shoulder; there was nobody there. She considered the last two sentences and then erased them. Her father wouldn't understand.

She shivered. This room was really too cold to sit in for long, nice though it was not to share with Jennifer for once. Gathering up her writing materials she took them downstairs, where she finished the letter to her father and wrote a long, cheerful one to her mother.

It had stopped raining after lunch. She discovered from Aunt Sylvia that the nearest mail box was in the village, and the younger ones said they would come with her, since they had discovered that the village shop sold candy.

"You'll go too, won't you, Frederick," said his mother firmly.

He might have gone anyway, but he disliked being managed.

Before they left Polly got Michael and Jennifer on their own for a moment upstairs. "Give Frederick some of your candy, won't you? He doesn't get any spending money."

"Why not?"

"I suppose it's because they're strict with him, or something."

Frederick was astonished by the number of offerings he received on the way back from the village.

"No, no, I can't take the last one," he protested to Jennifer.

"Oh please do," she urged nobly, and wore a happily martyred expression afterwards. She was overdoing it, Polly feared.

"Carry Number Three for me," instructed Hugh presently, handing him over.

"No," said Polly, giving him back. "If you bring him out, you must look after him."

"I'm tired." He wilted so that the bear dragged in the dust.

"You're wearing his feet out. Don't be so cruel," said Polly.

He lifted him up. "Tell us a story."

"Oh yes, tell us a story," exclaimed Michael and Jennifer.

"Not now," said Polly.

"Oh please, please do."

"I can't. It would be boring for Frederick."

"No it wouldn't," he said truthfully. He wanted to see what kind of story she told.

"Well, all right. After all, you don't have to listen." She thought for a few moments; then, with a sudden inspiration, began: "Once, a long while ago, a family lived in Frederick's house with one son and one daughter. And the daughter met a handsome young man and fell in love with him; but her parents didn't like him because he was poor. When he asked if he could marry her they were very angry and said she wasn't to see him any more. So she ran away with him; and the parents were so angry they disinherited her—that means they said she wasn't their daughter any more—and her brother was very angry too."

"Why? It had nothing to do with him," said Jennifer.

"Don't interrupt. Where was I? Oh yes, well, they didn't care; they got married, and she had a baby, a girl called Sarah. . . ."

As they reached the gate she was saying ". . . and he went out of the kitchen. Look, we're home."

"And then?" said Frederick.

"Well . . . she took the drink out to Thugdon, and this time he didn't growl or anything. To be continued," she finished grandly.

"What a funny place to stop. Go on," said Frederick.

"No, I can't until I've made up some more."

"You made that up just now," Jennifer observed.

"I can't do any more today," reiterated Polly, and felt slightly guilty at her evasion of the truth.

4 ❧ *A Sound of Crying*

Uncle Clement didn't go to work on Saturday. At lunch time he came in from the garden rubbing his hands and beaming.

"Lovely weather, just the ticket," he said. "I'll take you youngsters for a drive this afternoon. How about that? Think you can all pile into the car, if some sit on others' knees?"

"What a good idea," said Aunt Sylvia cheerfully.

"I don't think I'll come," said Frederick. "It'll be a good opportunity to get some of my summer reading done. I haven't looked at it yet."

"Oh come now, there'll be plenty of time for that when your guests have gone home," said his father.

They were hardly *his* guests, thought Frederick, since he hadn't invited them, and hadn't wanted them, either. "There'll be more room if I don't come."

"Actually," mentioned Polly uneasily, "I get car sick."

"Oh, what a shame. Still, in that case it's just as well

if Frederick stays at home, too," said Uncle Clement briskly. "He'll be company for you. That is if he doesn't insist on stifling in his room all afternoon."

"And you'll have space to give me a lift into town," said Aunt Sylvia.

Luckily the younger children were pleased and excited about the trip, and went off waving at the two who were left behind.

"What shall we do?" asked Frederick gloomily.

"You can do what you like. I'm going to lie on the lawn and read a book."

"Oh." He looked so taken aback that she laughed.

"It isn't my fault that I've got to stay too, but I won't interfere with your plans for working."

"I'll bring it out on the lawn," he compromised.

They settled themselves comfortably, Frederick choosing a patch of shade.

"You'll get a headache if you try to read with the sun on your back like that," he said.

"No, I like sun."

"What it really was," he said after a few minutes, "I don't like drives. They bore me."

"Because you've always had a car, I suppose. It's a thrill for the young ones; it would be for me, too, if I didn't get ill."

After half an hour Frederick got up. "I can't concentrate," he complained. "Insects keep walking over my book, and the wind blows the pages over, and the ground's so hard. I think I'll go up to my room if you don't mind."

"I said I didn't," replied Polly, not bothering to look up.

The warmth beating down on her was making her drowsy, and presently she abandoned her book and pillowed her face on her arms. She would try to invent a continuation of the Sarah story; Michael and Jennifer had been pestering her about it for days.

At that moment Michael and Jennifer were happily driving along beside a huge reservoir.

"They drowned a village to make this," said Uncle Clement.

"All the people?" asked Hugh, interested.

"Haha! No, the inhabitants moved out first. They say you can sometimes hear the bells of the drowned church ringing—but that's only a story, of course."

"Polly told us a story once about a house by a lake," said Michael. "The butler was haunted by a green hand that kept tapping on the window of his pantry."

"He had a special pantry all to himself," put in Jennifer.

"And when he went down into the cellar there were slimy footprints on the floor."

"Really?" said their uncle. "Look, you see those things sticking up? If the surface of the water gets too high, it runs away down those holes. Do you see?"

"Yes," said Michael. "And when we were undressing that night something tapped on our window, something green—"

"And Polly said 'a green hand!'" took up Jennifer. "We *were* scared."

"It wasn't a green hand, of course," said Uncle Clement firmly.

"No, it was a spray of ivy," admitted Michael. "But another time we heard a funny tapping in the bedroom and we didn't know *what* it was, and we called Polly in—"

"And it had stopped when she came, and she said, 'If you're a ghost, tap again,' and it went dadada da."

"We all rushed downstairs."

"You left me behind," remarked Hugh.

"You were in bed."

"I heard you all run away."

"When the weather is very dry," said Uncle Clement, "the water gets so low that you can actually see the church tower."

"I can't," said Hugh.

"No, not now, but if the water was lower you could."

"Oh," said Hugh vacantly, and began to suck his thumb.

"It was Captain making the tapping noise," resumed Michael tenaciously. "He haunts our attic. He's a little old man with a stick."

"Sometimes when Polly's upstairs on her own she hears him whisper her name."

Uncle Clement gave up hope of changing the subject. "Did Polly tell all of you about him? Hugh, too?"

"Yes," said Hugh lugubriously, removing his thumb. "I think it's funny. It makes me laugh."

"Haha! Yes, Polly should really choose an older house to tell her stories about. No sea captains have lived or died in yours, I'm afraid."

Hugh had stopped listening, but Michael said in a troubled tone, "Captain *is* there. Polly said so. She didn't say he used to live there—she says he's there now."

"Alive?" asked Uncle Clement banteringly. "A real captain?"

"Not ordinary alive," said Michael.

"Polly is obviously a good story-teller."

After that they didn't tell him any more.

Polly had gone to sleep on the lawn. When she woke she was in the shade, and felt cold, stiff and slightly damp. She stood up and moved out of it; but even the sun wasn't as warm as it had been.

Then to her surprise she heard a faint sound of crying. She looked around her. Nothing moved among the trees, and it almost seemed as though it must be coming from the house. She moved slowly across the lawn and the crying grew slightly louder. Embarrassed, she glanced up at Frederick's closed window. Was he crying behind it, and if so, why? The boys who called him Fred might perhaps sneer at him for being a drudge, but would they also say sissy? He hadn't struck her as the kind of boy who would give way to tears.

Perhaps something really dreadful was wrong? She couldn't decide whether or not to go and see. He must realize she could hear him. Maybe he was ill, in which case surely she ought to do something to help.

The crying seemed to stop as soon as she went into the kitchen, but as she approached the stairs she heard it again, low, half-choked sobs with a most miserable sound to them. She had better knock at his door and say something like, "Fluff, are you all right?"

As she reached the landing the sobbing broke off. He must have heard her coming. So perhaps she ought to go away again; or better, she could visit him and pretend not to know anything about it.

"Can I come in?" she asked cheerfully.

"Yes, do," he called, and looked up from his desk with a welcoming expression. "Are you hungry? I was just thinking it must be nearly time for a snack."

"Yes," said Polly weakly. "I suppose it must." His face was quite dry and he was perfectly composed; however did he manage it?

"Let's go and see what we can find. I don't think we have to wait for the others," he said, putting his books in a neat pile.

"Yes."

"You sound a little dazed. Do you think you've stayed in the sun too long?"

Polly burst out: "Are you all right?"

"I merely asked a reasonable question," he said stiffly.

"There's no need to go all offended. I didn't mean that. But weren't you, well, crying a bit just now?"

He looked at her blankly. "Of course I wasn't."

"I heard crying."

"What would I cry for? Don't be silly, Polly."

"I heard crying," she repeated emphatically. "I came in to see what was wrong. If it wasn't you, *you* must have heard it too."

"I haven't heard anything. You must have been mistaken."

"But I tell you I heard it."

"It was something else you heard. It obviously didn't come from inside the house. Maybe it was doves in the trees."

"They don't cry, they coo. Besides it did, it came from an upstairs room. It only stopped when I reached the landing."

"Well, do I look as though I've been crying?"

"No," said Polly slowly. "You don't. I believe you, that's what makes it so horrid."

"Charming, I'm sure."

"Fluff, please be serious. If it wasn't you, who was it?"

"That's easily answered. It must have been a ghost."

"But you don't believe in ghosts," she said uneasily.

"I don't, but you do. And you'd like me to, wouldn't you?"

"Do you think I'm just making this up to frighten you?" If anyone was frightened, she thought indignantly, it was herself.

Frederick drew back in the face of her vehemence. "No, I suppose not; but then you must have imagined it."

Polly gave up in despair. She couldn't eat much, although Frederick urged food on her most politely. She kept going over what had happened in her mind, and trying not to dwell on his derisive suggestion of a ghost.

Then the others came home, having picked up Aunt Sylvia on their way.

"We had a lovely time, Polly, you should have come," said Michael. "We saw a ruined tower and the entrance to a cavern and a big lake that's on top of a village and sometimes you can still hear the church bells ringing."

"Yes, quite a successful outing," beamed Uncle Clement. "Pity you two stayed behind. Did you have an enjoyable afternoon?"

"It was to start with. Well, most of it was," said Polly.

"Oh?" Uncle Clement's eyebrows rose.

"Something funny happened."

"Funny peculiar or funny ha ha?"

"Peculiar. I heard a sound of crying, coming from upstairs."

"Which she thought was me," said Frederick brightly.

"Yes, but it wasn't. And there wasn't anyone else there."

The younger ones were listening too. Michael said seriously: "This house is old enough to be haunted."

"This house isn't haunted. I've lived here six years and I know. Now go and wash your hands before supper," said Uncle Clement with cheerful firmness. As soon as they had gone his expression changed.

"Polly, what you do when you're at home is your parents' affair, but while you're staying here I wish you wouldn't terrify your little brothers and sister with grisly tales about this house. All right?"

"I forgot they were listening," said Polly. "It is really haunted then?"

"What are you talking about? Of course it's not. You just heard me say so."

"But that was to Michael. Oh, I see. You think I imagined it too."

"You did look odd when you came in, you know,"

said Frederick kindly. "I suspect it was too much sun."

"I hadn't been in the sun," protested Polly. "I went to sleep and it moved off me. I was quite cold."

"Well, there you are!" said Uncle Clement. "You dreamed it."

"No, I was awake when I heard it. I heard it all the way up the stairs." She added, "You did say you believed in ghosts."

Uncle Clement sighed. "I said perhaps, and I wouldn't even have said that if I'd realized what a wild imagination you've got. Did Frederick hear this, er, ghost?"

"No," said Frederick.

"Well, Polly? What are we to make of that?"

"I don't know," she said unhappily.

"I should just forget about it as quickly as possible if I were you," advised Uncle Clement.

Polly hoped she would be able to. Thinking over some of the things he had said, she asked Michael later, "Did you tell Uncle about the stories I tell you?"

"Yes, and we told him about Captain. Polly, he said our house isn't old enough to be haunted. Isn't Captain real?"

"Well . . . he might be."

"You mean he's not," said Michael sadly.

"Do you like him then? Doesn't he terrify you?"

"Only nicely." He sounded very disappointed. Then he brightened. "Is this house haunted?"

"No," said Polly without pausing to think.

"What about that crying you heard?"

"Doves," said Polly, "in the trees."

On reflection she thought she had said the best thing.

Captain was a homely sort of ghost, really; but unexplained crying was a different matter.

Uncle Clement was so genial at dinner that she felt bold enough to ask: "If the house isn't haunted, might the pool be?"

"Oh, Polly." He laid down his knife and fork with a weary expression. "Do you mean the lake?"

"No, the little pool up behind the house."

"Little, yes indeed—you might just as well suggest a haunted puddle."

"Something frightened us there."

"Come on then, let's hear this one."

The sight of his and Frederick's faces made Polly want to drop the subject, but she had gone too far now. "We were exploring the wood, and when we got up to where the pool is we found we were whispering, without meaning to; and then suddenly we all felt very scared and ran away."

"You didn't hear anything this time?"

"No," said Polly, reddening.

"Unexplained panic in woods is a very common phenomenon, you know, Polly. It was once thought to be fear of the god Pan—hence the word panic."

"That's interesting," said Frederick.

"I've experienced it myself on occasion."

"By the pool?" asked Polly swiftly.

"No, not by the pool. In very much larger woods than these, as a matter of fact."

"Oh." She felt slightly snubbed; but she admitted to herself that she was also reassured by his words.

5 ❦ Sarah's Letter

Next day Uncle Clement drove the five children to church while Aunt Sylvia cooked lunch. Michael and Jennifer came out to the car quarreling about who would sit in the front seat.

"You can share it," said Uncle Clement, "and the other three will fit nicely into the back."

Neither was particularly pleased with this arrangement, but they didn't argue. Polly sat by an open window; Frederick, shivering, by a closed one; and Hugh bounced up and down in the middle.

The village church was a pretty little graystone building with a spire.

The minister was very tall, with a head of unruly black hair and a surprisingly young face. He seemed to find it difficult to be dignified; taking the chancel steps too fast, he tripped over the hem of his robe, and his long arms waved as he recovered his balance. Uncle Clement clicked his tongue disapprovingly.

Because she liked the look of him Polly listened

harder than usual to the sermon, and in fact she had never heard one so interesting before. She felt really annoyed with Hugh for playing all the while with the hymn books, and when he dropped one and burrowed noisily after it she hoisted him back by the ear and told him sharply to behave. Uncle Clement frowned at both of them.

When they came out afterwards the minister was in the vestibule.

"I liked your sermon," said Polly boldly.

He bent a rather worried smile in her direction. "Did you? And let me see, you are . . ."

"My niece, Polly Devenish," boomed Uncle Clement, his hand descending on her shoulder from behind. "Polly, our minister, Mr. Mather."

"How do you do, Polly," said the minister gravely.

"Howjado," mumbled Polly, and sliding away from her uncle's hand she went out into the sunshine to look at the graves.

Some were very sad: "Thomas, aged five," and one to a young wife: "Her sun has gone down while it was yet day." There was a stone to Grace, Emily and James, who had died in the same year, aged six, three and one: "Till the day break," it said, and Polly, eyes watering, felt sure their parents had had no other children. The biggest monument of all was white marble, two angels holding an open book inscribed "The souls of the righteous are in the hands of God." This one was to Simon Stampenstone, who had died in 1900, aged forty-five. Too old to be interesting, thought Polly.

"Come on, you ghoul," said Frederick, appearing beside her. "We're all waiting in the car."

"Oh, I'm sorry. I thought Uncle was talking to the minister. Have you ever looked at these graves?"

"No, I'm not interested in dead people."

When they got home there was a delicious smell of roasting meat to greet them.

"Polly complimented Mather on his sermon," said Uncle Clement.

"Did you, dear?" Aunt Sylvia gave her a faintly incredulous smile.

"I sometimes wonder if he's quite suitable for this parish."

"I believe the Ladies' Auxiliary gets along well with him."

"All the same, it's a pity he's not married."

Since they were talking as though she wasn't there, Polly went away.

Early the next day the first long stripes of sunlight lay across the garden and touched the sill in Polly's room. But she lay sleeping; and in her dream an alarm clock had just awakened her to the black cold of a winter morning at six o'clock. She was Sarah again.

She got out of bed, lit her candle, and after washing rather skimpily in ice-cold water put her clothes on as fast as possible to warm herself up. Her uncle had told her Mrs. Piper arrived at half past six, and Sarah was already in the kitchen when she let herself in through the back door. She had a rosy, screwed-up little face and bright brown eyes like a squirrel's.

"Good morning," said Sarah timidly.

"Oh 'allo dear, are you Sarah?" she responded in cheerful cockney tones. "Mr. Stampenstone's told me all about you. Well, sit down dear, might as well rest our legs while we can, and I'll tell you what we'll be doing. First we 'ave to get the stove lit, clean the grates, light the fires, and do out the study. Then 'e gets up and we cook the breakfast. Now 'ave you ever cleaned a grate, dear?"

"No."

"Well, I'll show you 'ow and you can be getting on with it while I light the stove, else there'll be no 'ot water for 'im to wash with. Got an apron, dear?"

Sarah fetched her brown homespun pinafore.

"That's fine, dear. Don't want to spoil yer good dress, do you?"

Miss Swirles had kindly made the dress out of some old curtains of hers; she had done all she could to help Sarah after her mother died.

"Does my—he go to work in the daytime?" Sarah didn't dare refer to him as her uncle now, and Mrs. Piper's "he" seemed the best alternative.

"No, dear. 'E sits in 'is study. 'E's a writing gentleman. Tracts and that."

"What time do you go?" asked Sarah a little wistfully. She thought she would much rather work under Mrs. Piper's instruction than be left alone with her uncle.

"Twelve, dear. Now you just take the ashes out to the bin."

The lid of the bin clattered as Sarah took it off, and she heard from among the trees a volley of warning barks. Thugdon came bounding across the lawn and circled round her, changing his serious tone to an occasional exclamation and baring his teeth in a great red grin. She took a step towards the back door, eyeing him warily and wondering if he would let her reach it in safety. He came no closer, however.

"That great animal," said Mrs. Piper when she returned. "Bother you, did 'e? No, 'e is quite well be'aved. The size of 'im, though. An' eats like I dunno what—costs as much to feed 'im as though 'e was 'uman. Funny 'im spending money on an animal that way—'e's mean enough in most things, 'Eaven knows." It took Sarah a moment to realize that the "he" in the last sentence was not the dog.

The time went quickly, until suddenly Mrs. Piper glanced at the clock and said in a flurry: "Look at that, I'm all be'ind, and 'e'll be down in a minute and breakfast not laid—" She broke off, looking thoughtful. "'Ere's a thing now. Do you 'ave your breakfast with '*im*, or what?"

"We had our meal together last night, but I'd really rather not . . ." said Sarah anxiously.

Before they could come to a decision they heard Mr. Stampenstone's step on the stairs.

"Good morning, Mrs. Piper. Is breakfast ready?"

"Good morning, sir; well not quite. I've been a bit slowed down on account of showing Miss Sarah—"

"You may omit the Miss, she's not your employer." His eyes swiveled to Sarah, who immediately became conscious of her hot, untidy state. "Sarah. Go and take off that garment, wash the dirt off your face, and comb your hair. Then perhaps you'll be fit to appear at the breakfast table." The contempt in his voice brought tears to her eyes; she turned her back quickly and hurried away.

After a silent meal he shut himself into the study and Sarah found she was expected to become a servant again. Mrs. Piper, a little subdued at first, was soon talking as much as ever except when in earshot of the study. Sarah worked hard and felt very tired when the morning was over.

She seemed free to do what she liked in the afternoon. She went upstairs, thinking it would cheer her up to write to Miss Swirles; but when she reached her room the letter was forgotten as she gazed blankly at the naked blankets on her bed. Her mother's shawl had disappeared.

She began to tremble. She couldn't ignore its disappearance; but she didn't feel brave. She whispered, "Help me," in a kind of prayer to her mother, and went down to knock on the study door.

"Come in," he said irritably. "What do you want? I'm busy."

"Please, sir, I'm sorry to bother you, but have—have you taken the shawl from my bed?"

He looked coldly astonished. "And if I have?"

Sarah struggled for words. "Please—may I have it back, sir? It—I value it."

"A strange use for something you value. It was quite out of place there, and I happen to value it rather more."

"But—sir, it—it's mine. It was my mother's—"

"It was *my* mother's. It came from this house, do you understand that? It was a completely unsuitable possession for you, and you had no right to it whatsoever."

"It was my mother's," muttered Sarah doggedly.

He stood up and towered over her with a frown.

"What have I told you about mentioning her? Leave this room at once."

Sarah half turned, but she still couldn't quite give up. "Sir, please—please let me have it back. I will promise to take care of it, I'll keep it in a drawer—"

"Leave the room," he said, and held open the door with terrible politeness. She went.

When she had cried away some of her rage and desolation she began her letter to Miss Swirles.

I arrived here safely. It is a very lonely house with trees all around. Uncle Simon keeps a big fierce dog to guard it. I am not allowed to call him Uncle, because he says my mother was disinherited so I am not his relation. I think I see now why my mother never wrote to him. I think he must have hated her.

He says I must be a servant, and I am learning how from Mrs. Piper, who comes every morning. She seems friendly. I don't think she likes him much either. This morning when he came down to breakfast he was angry with me for being in a pinafore and having a dirty face, but if I am to do housework how can I help looking like that? I have to use the back door like Mrs. Piper.

Did you ever see Mother's Indian shawl that she liked so much, she said it was the only pretty thing she had. I brought it here with me and put it on my bed and he has just taken it away, he says I can't have it, he says it isn't mine because it was their mother's first. I know Mother wanted me to have it. He said it shouldn't be on my bed.

I wish I was back at school. You have been so kind already, maybe you will write to me.

The last two paragraphs narrowly escaped being blotched with tears. She blew her nose and sealed the letter; then realized she had no stamps and no money. She would have to ask *him;* it was an unattractive thought.

"I wonder if I might have a stamp, sir?" They had nearly finished their supper before she plucked up courage to say it.

"A stamp? For what?"

"A—a letter to my old schoolteacher, sir."

"Miss Hogwash? What d'you want to write to her for, eh?"

Sarah had not seen him in this jovially brutal mood before. She said faintly: "She is a friend, sir. She was very good to me when—she has always been very good."

"Oh, very well, I'll stamp your letter to this saint. Has Mrs. Piper taught you how to wash china yet?"

"Yes sir." (In fact she had accepted Sarah's assurance that she already knew.)

"Wash these things, then." He rose abruptly, indicating the table. "Bring me the letter before you begin."

She did as she was told. She had dried the china and was putting it away when he came into the kitchen, an opened envelope in one hand and her letter dangling from the other. After one glance, fright and indignation stopped her tongue. He gave her no time to speak in any case.

"This *missive.* What do you mean by it? How some-

one your age could be so wickedly ungrateful—I find
it quite unbelievable." His voice began to rise. "Not
content with slandering me in every direction, you
accuse good Mrs. Piper of disloyalty to her employer.
Well? What have you to say for yourself?"

"I—didn't suppose you would read it, sir."

"Didn't suppose I would read it! No, I dare say you
didn't! The impudence of your attempting to slide it
out under my very nose! I don't know how you have
been brought up previously, but let me tell you now
that girls of your age are not usually allowed to send out
letters that have not been read by a responsible adult—
where one is available. I trust you can see how necessary
this precaution is, in view of what has just occurred!"

"Sir," assented Sarah woodenly.

"Take it," he said with disgust, letting it drop. "Burn
it."

Sarah retrieved it and laid it silently on the glowing
coals of the range. There was a puff of flame, and it
turned to ash.

"Next time," he said over his shoulder, "you will be
punished."

Sarah left the kitchen tidy and went up to her room.
She took a sheet of paper and rewrote her letter, as far
as she could remember it. She added another paragraph:

I have written this letter once already. I gave
it to him to stamp for me and he opened it and read
it. He was very angry, he said I was ungrateful.
He said he would read all my letters. He made me
burn it. I shall mail this myself. I am sorry I can't
pay for it.

She put it in an envelope and wrote in the corner *To Be Paid For On Arrival.* Then she hid it under her mattress, and went to bed.

Next day her uncle said to Mrs. Piper: "If you show Sarah how to prepare his meals, she can feed Thugdon in the future."

"Oh it's all right, sir, it's no trouble to me to do him," Mrs. Piper replied cheerfully. "I'm used to him."

He frowned. "I wish Sarah to do it. It will be good for her."

After he had gone Mrs. Piper said: "Do you mind, dear? 'E is a big dog, but 'e's never 'urt anyone so far's I know. Course, you got to watch Alsatians—I wouldn't trust most of 'em farther'n I could throw 'em."

This left Sarah little comforted. She thought her uncle must have had the idea to punish her for her letter.

" 'E 'as 'is own meat, it's kept 'ere. You cut it up in lumps like this, see, enough to fill 'is bowl—and look, I keep this jam jar for taking water out to fill 'is other bowl. It's quite simple reely."

"Yes, I see."

Sarah wondered if she dared leave the house this afternoon without asking permission, but decided she didn't.

"May I go for a walk today, sir?" she asked while they ate their lunch.

"Haven't you anything useful to do? No, I suppose not. Well, Satan finds work . . . it's a harmless way of using up your energies. Yes, you may."

"Thank you, sir." She was relieved at its being so easy, but she didn't really feel safe until she had washed the lunch things and fetched her coat, and was walking along the drive. Then she was scared by the sudden approach of Thugdon, silent for once. He pranced along near her until she reached the road and stood in the gateway to watch her depart, uttering a couple of deep, resonant barks. She was glad to be free of him so easily.

It was good to be free of the house as well, out on her own in the sunshine. It was a clear, cold day. In a field by the road cows were eating a load of cabbage which had been scattered for them; farther away someone was ploughing. There were still one or two withered black-berries on the brambles, but they were, as she discovered, completely inedible. A flight of rooks passed overhead and settled among the new furrows.

Nobody much was about in the village. She saw a woman taking food to some hens, and passed an old man shuffling along with a stick. He smiled at her. As she went by the little stone school a sound of chanting made her homesick for Miss Swirles's classroom. She found a mail box quite easily, dropped her letter inside, and began to return slowly along the way she had come.

Before she had gone far Polly woke up.

6 ✤ A Visit to Mr. Mather

"I'm so glad I'm me and not her," she thought sleepily. She thought it several times.

Then, as her head cleared, she began to feel an increasing astonishment. "It's not the first time you've dreamed about the same people twice," she told herself sensibly. No, but she'd never had two dreams before that dovetailed so exactly. She had dreamed she was other people, but usually she was herself too, watching from outside as though reading a book. And dreams, however sensible they seemed while she was having them, turned out to have been absurd when she woke. They were bound to. ("That's how you know real life isn't a dream," she thought confusedly.) Only this dream, these dreams, didn't. Sarah was just like a real person; it was horrible to find she had just lived two days of someone else's life.

"Well then," thought Polly, "I dreamed a night. She —I—must have gone to sleep. How can you dream you're asleep? What did it feel like?" But on reflection she concluded that there had been a gap at that point; nothing unusual, in a dream. The gap had lasted until that vile uncle came and said Sarah was to feed Thugdon. (Another odd thing. Polly loved dogs herself.) All the second day had been rather spotty, in fact. But she was glad Sarah had managed to get the letter mailed in spite of Mr. Stampenstone—she sat up in bed, shivering with excitement. Simon Stampenstone was real. He was buried in the village churchyard. She had seen his grave.

Frederick had got up early that morning; the new microscope catalogue he was expecting had arrived, and he was engrossed in it at the kitchen table when Polly came in.

"Hello, Fluff," she said in the tones of one who means to be heard.

He didn't want to talk; he half looked up and said: "Hello. Juice in the pitcher."

Polly brushed that aside. "It's a lovely day; let's go for a little walk round the garden."

He didn't really think the continuing dry weather called for such enthusiasm, and couldn't she see he was busy? "What, now?"

"Go on, Frederick, it'll give you an appetite," said Uncle Clement, coming in with an empty coffee cup.

The catalogue was too floppy to slam shut, or Frederick would have done so. He scraped his chair back and stood up slowly. "Where d'you want to go?"

"Just out."

It was quite pleasant in the garden, but he wouldn't admit so to Polly.

"Don't be cross, Fluff," she cajoled. "I wanted to tell you something. I haven't told anyone else."

Nor would he admit that his interest was aroused. Instead he said ironically: "Have I got to promise not to tell, either?"

"No, but I would rather you didn't. Fluff, I keep having dreams about people who used to live in this house."

"What people?" He was disappointed; this was Polly in her silly mood.

"That Sarah girl and her uncle."

"Oh, you mean pretend people. What's funny about that?"

"No, you don't understand. They weren't pretend, I dreamed them. That's why I didn't go on with the story, because that's all I'd dreamed then; but now I've dreamed some more."

"Well—good," said Frederick, and added, making an effort: "I expect the little ones will be pleased. I won't tell them you don't make it up."

"But, Fluff, the dreams are so sensible, and the people, at any rate Sarah's uncle, are real. He's Simon Stampenstone."

"And she's Sarah Stampenstone, I suppose," said Frederick flippantly.

"No, Gray. Her mother was his sister." She stopped and looked suspicious. "Fluff, you're not taking me seriously."

"Have you said anything serious yet?"

"I tell you he's Simon Stampenstone. You must have seen his grave, the one with the big white thingamajig."

"The one you were looking at on Sunday?" He was suddenly alert. "Truthfully? Is that really the name on it? It doesn't say he lived *here* though, does it?"

"No, but I bet he did. The dreams get things right. The house is right, but different furniture. The village is right, but less houses."

"What a clever dreamer you are."

"But it isn't me. I don't know these things. How could I?"

"You must admit it's just your kind of dream. Happenings from the murky past. The name could be a coincidence."

"A name like that?"

"Well," said Frederick judicially, "unless you can prove he did once live here—"

"I will. You wait and see." They had come close to the lake and she stopped and looked at it. "We could have fun with a boat here."

"We haven't got one, and if we had it wouldn't be safe. You could easily drown."

"I can swim."

"Can the others?"

"We don't have to take them in the boat."

"There isn't a boat," he reiterated.

"Could anyone drown in the pool?" she wondered idly.

"Of course they couldn't, you idiot."

"Not even a very small person?" She was arguing for the sake of it, but:

"Come and see for yourself, then perhaps you'll believe me," he said, adding swiftly, "unless you're scared, that is."

She did believe him, but she recognized that she was being dared. "All right."

She would be unlikely to panic in Federick's company. She didn't really see why the wood should frighten her at all. She liked it so: the sound of birds and the piney smell, the cushion grass and the brilliant green moss.

All the same, when they reached the pool she wished she hadn't come. It was somehow too serene and beautiful here; she felt herself wanting to whisper again.

"There, you see?" said Frederick. "But I'll prove it to you quite definitely. No cheating." He found a piece of stick and approached the water.

"Don't bother," said Polly hastily. "I can see you're right."

"It's not altogether fair, though, because water is always deeper than it looks."

"Yes, I know. Please don't—don't interfere with it, Fluff." She didn't know why she pleaded so urgently.

"For heaven's sake!" he exclaimed, and carefully immersed the stick. Before he could withdraw it she had gone, running down the hill.

Life with Polly was impossible, he thought angrily, as he followed at a normal pace. She turned everything into a melodrama. Well, he would just refuse to play. He wouldn't say a word when he caught up with her.

Actually, even if he had asked, she wouldn't have told him why she had fled. It was such a silly reason that she barely admitted it even to herself; but when he had disturbed the pool, she had felt that a third person stood behind them—someone who disapproved.

They entered the house separately and found the younger ones halfway through their breakfast. Uncle Clement had already left for work.

"Who lived here before you did?" Polly asked her aunt.

"What odd things you come out with. . . . Some people called Brown, I think it was."

"Did some Stampenstones ever live here?"

"I really don't know. . . . Michael, I'd rather you didn't give your crusts to the cat, dear."

Polly glared at him and pressed on, undaunted by her aunt's bored expression. "There's a Simon Stampenstone buried in the churchyard; he has white marble angels holding a book."

"Yes, I believe I've noticed," murmured Aunt Sylvia.

"Who would know where he lived, if you don't?"

"The minister might." She gave a little yawn and left the room quickly, as though she had remembered something she had to do. It looked like an escape to Frederick. He buried himself in his catalogue, pretending he hadn't listened to the conversation.

Polly managed to slip away on her own after breakfast. She wasn't sure that her aunt's suggestion had been serious, but it was worth a try.

Frederick found to his annoyance that in Polly's absence he was expected to look after and entertain his younger cousins.

"Take them out," said his mother. "Mrs. Richards wants to clean this morning."

They wouldn't come until they had searched the whole house for Polly. Then they began on the garden.

"What makes you think she's hiding?" asked Frederick.

"She does at home," said Jennifer; and Frederick thought he didn't blame her.

"She might have climbed a tree," said Michael.

Once they got among the trees themselves their purpose was forgotten. They ran and climbed and chat-
tered incessantly, except for Hugh, whose mouth was
mostly plugged with thumb.

"Don't you know," said Frederick, irritated by this
habit, "that to little boys who suck their thumbs—"

Hugh withdrew it with a plop and recited expressionlessly, "The great tall tailor always comes before they
know what he's about he takes his great long scissors
out snip snap snip snap they go so fast that both his
thumbs are off at last."

"Don't you care?"

"No," said Hugh, and put it back.

Frederick felt he had descended, even if fruitlessly,
to Polly's level; he was somewhat ashamed of himself.

Presently they reached the boundary wall that ran
across the hill.

"Oh," said Jennifer, "we can't get any farther.
Which way shall we go now?"

"Left," said Frederick, choosing this direction because it would bring them eventually to the pool. He
had a fancy to see how they reacted to it without Polly
there.

They heard the stream before they saw it and Michael
realized what it meant.

"The pool was near the wall," he said, stopping.

"We didn't like the pool," said Jennifer, stopping too.

"You will today," insisted Frederick. "It's a nice
place."

"It frightened us."

"We ran away."

"Polly said it was an adventure."

"I don't like adventures like that."

"Hugh doesn't mind," Frederick pointed out. Hugh was stumping on alone.

"He wasn't there before." But they were beginning to waver.

"We'll just have a quick look at it," said Frederick; and they followed him in silence.

"Isn't it a nice place, Hugh?" he said when they reached it. Hugh said something indistinguishable through his thumb.

"It's all right." Michael sounded relieved. "Why did we get frightened before?"

"It's easy to be frightened by nothing in a wood," Frederick told them; but privately he thought their fear had been caught from Polly.

Polly herself meanwhile had just reached the parsonage and was knocking on the door. Mr. Mather opened it himself and bent towards her with the anxious smile she remembered.

"Oh, hello, er . . ."

"Polly," she said clearly.

"Polly, that's it," he exclaimed. "I'm hopeless at names, but I know who you are; you liked my sermon. Come in. Let's see, you're staying here, aren't you, with—what can I do for you?"

"I'm staying at Greystones," began Polly.

"It's the house with all the trees, isn't it? A bit oppressive, I should think. Look, no need to stand in the hallway. I've just made a jug of coffee, and it'll be getting cold. Come and sit down. Do you like coffee? Here are some cookies."

Polly sat and waited while he found mugs and poured the coffee. She took a cookie.

"There now," he said, smiling contentedly as he sat down himself. "Your compliment was very heartening, you know. Pity you don't live here. Still, it's pleasant to see you again. Haven't you several brothers and sisters?"

Polly related their names and ages.

"How did you get rid of them this morning?"

"I just left them behind. I suppose they're playing with Frederick."

"The young scientist?"

Polly grinned, but admitted: "He's nicer than he seems. Sometimes."

"I'm sure he is," said Mr. Mather quickly. "I didn't mean to sound so sarcastic. Have another cookie." He glanced at his watch, and saw that Polly had noticed. "Don't worry, I'm just making sure that we've plenty of time to drink the coffee. I want to get the things washed up before Mrs. Biggs, my housekeeper, gets back. She doesn't approve of mid-morning snacking."

"Why not?"

"Extra work."

"But if you do it all yourself?"

"She doesn't like me in the kitchen, either."

"Do you have to do what she says?"

"That's a good question . . . I don't like unnecessary quarrels, you see. And I manage very well, as you perceive. She always stays a long while at the shop, exchanging news, I suppose. And anyway, her regime won't last very much longer—" he broke off, gave her a rather sheepish smile, and said: "Look, I shouldn't have told you that. It slipped out."

"All right, I won't repeat it."

He seemed to want to continue, now that he had begun. "I'm getting married, you see."

"Uncle Clement will approve of that."

"Will he? Mmmm. A minister's wife is useful in a parish—and mine will be useful in the village, if not in quite the conventional way. Here's a picture of her." He fumbled in his wallet. "There."

"She's pretty," said Polly truthfully. "She looks cheerful."

"Mmm." He put it away again. He looked slightly worried.

"What did you mean about not in the conventional way?"

"She's going to teach in the village school," he said gloomily.

"Well, that doesn't matter, does it?"

"No. Of course it doesn't." He sat up straighter. "She's a good teacher, and she didn't want to give up her job. I didn't want her to, either. We've been waiting for her to get a job in the neighborhood, and this particular job will be open in September. Couldn't be better in one sense. I shall have to announce it soon." He looked gloomy again.

"But what is the matter, then?"

"Well, it's . . . an unusual thing for a minister's wife to do. People may think it isn't suitable."

"They're just silly, then," said Polly roundly. "It sounds like a lovely arrangement to me."

He grinned. "Let's hope they think so, too. Finished your coffee? I don't want to hurry you, but—" He was looking at his watch again.

"Come on, I'll dry for you," said Polly, getting up.

He seemed surprised but pleased. "Well, thank you. That's most kind. The kitchen's this way."

"About what I came for . . ." began Polly, picking up a dish towel.

"Good Lord!" He dropped a mug and swooped after it, grabbing it just short of the floor. "How rude of me, I've talked about myself all the while, and quite forgot you must have a reason for calling. Do go on, I am sorry."

"It's just I want to know where someone who's buried in the churchyard lived. It's to settle a kind of bet."

"Really? Who?"

"Simon Stampenstone; he has the big white marble stone with angels."

"Yes, I can look that up for you in the parish records. I'll do it now, we've finished here. Come out of the kitchen in case Mrs. Biggs returns."

She followed him to the door of his study, and presently he said: "He left instructions for it, and money, before he died. Rather a smug inscription to choose . . . yes, he lived at Greystones. That's where you're staying, isn't it? I hope that means you've won the bet."

"Yes," said Polly, "it does. Thank you very much."

7 ★ Sarah's Punishment

"Oh, you're back, are you?" said Aunt Sylvia. "Please don't go out for so long again without telling anyone where you've gone. Where have you been?"

"To see Mr. Mather."

"What on earth for?"

"Well," said Polly reluctantly, "you said he'd know about the grave."

Her aunt stared; then gave a cool little laugh. "Nothing wrong with your nerve, is there?"

Polly realized that this was not a compliment and made no reply. She began to give the others some of the candy she had bought at the village shop.

"Here you are, Fl—Frederick."

"Oh, thank you," he said in surprise; then he realized he would have to stop being angry with her now, and added: "What did Mr. Mather say?"

The younger ones had run away. Polly said: "Simon Stampenstone did live here."

"Really?!" He was interested at last. "So you were

right after all. Well, how peculiar. Did you tell him why you wanted to know?"

"No, I said we had a bet on it."

Frederick nodded approvingly. "I never heard of anything quite like this before. Oh and by the way, you didn't tell me what happened in your latest dream."

"The others will want to hear too. Children!" shouted Polly. "I'm going to tell some more of the Sarah story!"

They came hurrying back.

"Do you remember where I'd got to? Well. Next morning . . ."

It was Uncle Clement's habit to sit in his favorite armchair before dinner with a glass of sherry. He was glancing through a newspaper when Polly and Frederick came in, but as they plumped down in chairs near his he politely put it aside.

"Daddy, did you know a man called Simon Stampenstone used to live in this house?"

"Well yes, as a matter of fact I did. Didn't you?"

"No," said Frederick, slightly crestfallen. "Neither did Mother."

"In that case I'm intrigued to know how you discovered it."

"Polly asked Mr. Mather. You see, she's been having these dreams. . . ."

Polly let him do the explaining; he put it so well. But it was to her that Uncle Clement turned with his question afterwards.

"So you think this is some kind of visitation from the past?"

"It's something, anyway," said Polly.

"What made you first think you might be dreaming about real people?"

"I saw his grave."

"Yes, it's rather ostentatious; you could hardly miss it, could you? Why didn't you ask Mr. Mather about it at once? I suppose you thought you'd try us first. Why did you leave me out of your inquiries, though?"

"Well, it was only this morning that I knew. In the first dream he was just Uncle Simon, but in last night's they said Mr. Stampenstone."

"Oh, Polly!" Uncle Clement began to laugh. "Prompt collapse of thesis, I'm afraid!"

"I never noticed that," exclaimed Frederick, annoyed with himself. Polly looked from one to the other uncomprehendingly.

"Look," said her uncle. "You saw the name on Sunday. On Sunday night you dreamed about it. Don't you think that might have been because the name was already in your head?"

Polly thought for a moment. "But he was called Simon in the first dream, before I saw the grave."

"Simon's not an unusual name. In fact, that was probably why you made the subconscious connection— two Simons."

"But," said Frederick slowly, "it didn't say on the grave that he'd lived here."

"You could have deduced it fairly easily," replied Uncle Clement after a slight pause. "It's obviously not a poor man's grave; and this is about the only house in the neighborhood, of sufficient age, big enough to be a likely home for him."

"Yes, but I didn't deduce it," protested Polly.

"I think your subconscious did," said Uncle Clement blandly.

"Yes," murmured Frederick, relieved. "That's certainly possible."

"Well . . ." said Polly. She felt confused.

"So I'm afraid you must relinquish your position as prophet of the past, hard though it is."

Polly felt a wave of dislike for him. "I suppose so," she muttered ungraciously; and then Aunt Sylvia brought the dinner in and the subject was closed.

Uncle Clement was unfair, Polly thought as she ate. She hadn't boasted about the dreams; she simply wanted them explained. And she couldn't quite believe that her subconscious (whatever that might be; she wasn't really sure) was capable of the feats he thought it had performed.

Perhaps it was because they had discussed them that she had another dream that night.

Sarah and Mrs. Piper sat at the kitchen table cleaning silverware.

"Got the 'ang of it now, 'aven't you, dear?"

Sarah looked down at the fork she was polishing. "I like seeing them brighten up."

"I don't mean just this, I mean all of it. There's not much more I can teach you. You're a grand little worker and that's the truth. Makes a big difference having you to 'elp me. There's a lot 'ere for one woman to get through mornings. I've told 'im, but 'e's not one to spend money if 'e can manage without. Well, I did get through; but jobs like this weren't done as often as they should've been. I shall miss you and that's a fact."

"It's kind of you to say so."

"No, I mean it, and it's not just the 'elp you are—I shall miss 'aving you to talk to. Still, it'll be better for you to get away. This 'ouse is too lonely for a young girl. Just because 'e never goes out 'imself, 'e never thinks as anyone else might want to.'

"He takes me to church on Sunday." A rapid march there and back, and inside the church she had quickly learned to keep her attention rigidly fixed on the service. He was aware of the slightest wandering of her eyes or turning of her head, and would silently crunch the bones above her elbow in a painful grip.

"Very nice too," said Mrs. Piper crisply, "but that's not the kind of thing I meant."

"I do go for walks," said Sarah with more feeling. "I enjoy that." She did, even though the cold drove her along at a smart pace and made her keep her hands in her pockets and wish for thicker boots.

"Eh, well, you're a solitary little creature. There, we've about finished these. I'll go and do the stairs if you'll peel the potatoes."

Sarah thought as she stood over the sink that she would miss Mrs. Piper also. She wondered if she would be working for anyone so cheerful and easy-going in her first job. Probably not; housekeepers in large establishments would naturally be much grander people. Her uncle had said nothing recently about her going away; she wondered if Mrs. Piper would tell him that she was ready now.

There was someone else she would miss, and that was Thugdon. They had grown fond of each other. After an early experiment, she knew better than to fondle him while he ate; but if she went on errands outside he always came up to have his head patted or his ears scratched. When she wasn't busy she often played with him, running races through the trees (which he won with ease) or throwing sticks for him to fetch. He particularly liked to retrieve them from the lake; and she enjoyed watching him as he swam, nose up and four legs stroking the water in a leisured, graceful movement just like walking. She thought he would have liked to accompany her on her walks, but he was too well trained to go beyond the gate. She could have asked her uncle's permission to take him with her, but she didn't think it would be granted; and she had a feeling that if he discovered she no longer feared Thugdon, he would even take the job of feeding him away from her.

When she had finished the potatoes she let the muddy water drain out of the peelings before taking them outside. Picking up a piece of cold pudding she had saved for Thugdon, who liked titbits, she carried it in her free hand. She didn't see him on her way to the bin, and on the way back she came face to face with her uncle, who had stepped outside the back door to look for her.

"What are you doing with that?" he asked at once, pointing to the pudding in her hand.

Luckily, or cleverly, Thugdon was keeping out of sight. "I—I was going to give it to the birds—sir."

"Birds?" Her uncle seemed to grow taller. "Birds? So now I'm expected to provide for birds of the air as well as penniless orphans, am I?"

"It's just—a piece that was left over, sir."

"I have eyes, girl. I can see what it is. Take it back into the kitchen. And understand this, Sarah." He gripped her shoulder fiercely. "I expect you to take as much care of my possessions as though they were your own. Otherwise you're no faithful servant."

Sarah thought that she wasn't his servant, anyway; then supposed drearily that she might as well be, for all the difference it made.

"I came to tell you you have received a letter." He took it out of his pocket and she gave a little start of nervousness. It was three weeks since she had mailed her letter to Miss Swirles, and she had begun to give up hope of a reply, though she still ran to pick up the letters when the mailman put them through the door. Today they must have come just while she was outside; and by an unfortunate chance her uncle must have emerged from his study at once to see what there was, a thing he seldom did.

"It seems to be from the town where you used to live," he said, looking at the postmark.

"Is it, sir?" She could see and recognize the writing now. It was from Miss Swirles.

"Whom do you think it might be from?"

"Perhaps—I don't know—a school friend, sir?" She dreaded the possibility of being told to open it in front of him.

"It looks to me like Miss Hogwash's hand," he said sharply, his eyes searching her face. Did he suspect something, or was he just playing with her? She couldn't think of anything at all to say.

"Come into my study," he ordered abruptly. "I shall read it to you."

"I—would rather read it myself, sir." But she knew it was useless.

"I dare say you would. I don't approve of that woman. Come along."

She followed him, trying not to tremble. He closed the study door behind him; then picked up a letter opener, slit the envelope, and took out the sheet of paper.

" 'My dear Sarah,' " he began in mocking tones, " 'I have been busy lately, and unable to write as soon as I should have liked. I was very distressed to hear' "—his voice took on a surprised depth—" 'of your unhappy situation. Your uncle is evidently—' " He broke off and read in silence, his face freezing. Sarah felt the palms of her hands running with moisture, and wiped them on her apron. He turned the page.

"Perhaps you would like to hear the last sentence," he said crisply. " 'Although it is undesirable that you should correspond with me against your uncle's wishes, the alternative, that you should be completely cut off from your friends, is worse.' Do you understand, Sarah? This woman, who calls herself your friend, is encouraging you in flagrant disobedience. The association must cease completely, do you understand me?" His voice grew louder and louder. The skin of his face was sucked in to make two white patches above his eyebrows.

"Answer me!"

"Yes, sir," she managed to say.

He glanced once more at the letter; then crumpled it in his fist. "The intervening portion consisted of sickly commiserations," he remarked briefly; then snapped:

"Go to your room and fetch your pen and writing paper. Hurry!"

Mrs. Piper was brushing the landing carpet.

"What's up, dear?" she asked, her eyes round with sympathy.

"I can't stop," Sarah jerked out as she hurried past.

When she returned with the things Mrs. Piper said: "Don't worry, dear." Sarah scarcely heard.

"Ink?" demanded Mr. Stampenstone.

"You didn't say—I'll fetch it, sir—"

"Use mine, use mine, you little fool. Close the door and come and sit here." He pointed to his desk and she obeyed him timidly, hating the drowned feeling she got in the big leather chair.

"Now take a piece of paper. You're about to write your last letter to Miss Hogwash, and it will be dictated by me." She didn't look up at him, but there was an unpleasant smile in his voice. "Ready? Write: Thank you for your letter. I have been thinking things over, and have prayed for guidance. I see how ungrateful and disobedient I have been, and shall not continue in the same wicked ways. It will be better if you do not write again. Yours, et cetera."

Sarah followed his dictation, but her hand was clumsy and shaking, and it was hard to make her writing legible.

"You're a poor advertisement for her precious school," he said contemptuously. "Put it in an envelope and address it." Sarah obeyed. "Now take your pen and the rest of your paper and put them on the fire. You'll have no further use for them."

It was hot, but Sarah went close and laid them gently in the flames; the little pile of smooth white sheets, the tooth-scarred pen whose splintery taste had often comforted her while she struggled with her sums. She wondered if the metal parts would melt, or whether she would find them among the ashes next day.

"Very well. There is one more thing. Did you mail that letter in the village?"

"Yes, sir."

"I thought so. Unstamped?"

"Yes, sir."

"A charming trick. In the future you don't leave the grounds, since you are not to be trusted outside them. Do you see this gong?" It hung on the wall. "I shall use it if I want to summon you back to the house. I warn you, don't let me find you out of earshot."

"No, sir." She knew she would never dare defy him in this.

"Now go to your room and stay there. And try to make what you have just written true!"

She left the room quickly, barely managing to contain tears until she was in her own. She sat huddled on the edge of her bed and cried because he had made her betray her friendship with Miss Swirles and because she wanted her mother and because she was alone. She cried until she had tired herself out.

Sometime later there was a knock, and a voice croaked softly: "It's only me, dear."

"Come in," called Sarah.

Mrs. Piper had a plate with her. " 'E said I was to bring you lunch before I left, dear. Well, I'm ashamed to bring it, I am reely. If 'e 'adn't 've kept 'is eye on me all the while you'd've got something different, I can tell you. 'E's the meanest devil alive and no mistake."

After a moment Sarah gathered her wits enough to recognize the piece of pudding that she had been going to give Thugdon. Somehow it provoked a rather watery smile.

"Well, but it's a shame, dear. What are you s'posed to 'ave done, anyway, if you don't mind me asking?"

Her small face was so red and creased with indignation that Sarah's tongue was loosened, and she began to pour everything out. She was crying again by the time she had finished. Mrs. Piper sat beside her on the bed and stroked her hand and repeated "There, dear; there, dear," over and over again.

"I'm sorry," murmured Sarah eventually; and straightening herself, she mopped her eyes.

"You needed a good cry, dear. You're 'aving the rough end of the stick and no mistake. You know, dear, like I said before, the sooner you go into service the better. Even if it's not what your poor mother would 'ave wanted—"

Sarah broke in with a slight gasp. "Did you know my mother?"

"Yes, dear." Mrs. Piper nodded firmly. "That I did, bless 'er 'eart. She was a little girl when I came 'ere from London. Mr. Stampenstone told me most particular before you came that I wasn't to mention 'er to you; but there's a time to disobey some orders."

"Did you work here when she lived here?"

"No, dear, they 'ad proper servants then; but I lived in the village, and I 'elped out at dinner parties and suchlike. This was a gay 'ouse in those days, and she was that pretty."

"Did you ever see my father?"

"Once or twice, dear. 'E was a very good-looking gentleman."

"I can't remember him. He died when I was three."

Mrs. Piper drew in her breath. "Eh, your poor mother. 'Owever did she manage?"

"She made clothes for people. It wasn't much money, but we did have enough. She always said she wouldn't ask my uncle for help; but when she . . . died, Miss Swirles said we must."

"Didn't she teach you dressmaking, then? It'd be a deal more suitable for you that what *'e's* planned."

"No, she never did; she hoped I might be a governess —but I wasn't very good at lessons. And I think she thought there would be time to teach me later, if . . ." Her voice trailed off, and she blew her nose.

"I've never forgotten 'ow 'appy she looked with 'im, the time or two I saw them," said Mrs. Piper quietly. "I used to wonder what became of them. It was all 'ushed up when they ran away, but I knew from Maria who worked 'ere. They were never mentioned afterwards, she said; it broke 'er parents' 'earts."

"Uncle Simon said that, too."

"Yes, well it didn't break 'is," snapped Mrs. Piper. She looked quite fierce. " 'E was always jealous of 'er, because she was their favorite, and no wonder, seeing as 'ow 'e was as sour as crabapples even as a lad. It just suited 'im when she ran off. 'E said everything 'e could to make them more upset—'e 'ad a proper twisty tongue. Old Mr. Stampenstone, 'e did that disin'eriting in a temper; but I'll bet Mr. Simon kept 'im feeling narked until 'e died, never gave 'im a chance to forgive 'er. 'E only lived a year after she left anyway; and Missis didn't last much longer, poor lady."

"I *thought* Uncle Simon must have hated her," breathed Sarah.

"I can tell you, when 'e told me you were coming to live 'ere I felt sorry for you at once. 'E's got a mean nature, and nobody could say different. It's just not in 'im to be kind to anyone. The only creature 'e's 'alfway kind to is that dog, and even the dog's afraid of 'im if you ask me. When 'e started saying I was to teach you 'ousework I knew 'ow it'd be. Nonsense about being poor—course 'e could afford to keep you if 'e wanted to. But like I said, p'r'aps it's a blessing in disguise 'e doesn't."

"Yes," said Sarah. "I've been thinking that for a long time."

"Eh, you poor little lass," Mrs. Piper sighed heavily. "I wish I could do something for you. I was right fond of your mother." She stood up slowly.

"You have done something," insisted Sarah, "talking about her to me. Thank you."

"I couldn't do less. Well, I must go, dear, but I'll see you tomorrow. Chin up now, and show 'im you don't care." She disappeared round the door with a jaunty little wave.

8 ❦ Gray One

When Polly woke next day she felt as if the dream still clung round her. It was an effort to come back to being herself. She ate her breakfast in silence, preoccupied with thoughts of Sarah. The only thing that penetrated her shell was a letter from home. She sat up and insisted on her right, as eldest, to read it first.

Their mother had had a good rest and was much better. They were to come home in a week's time. There was a letter to Aunt Sylvia, too.

Polly had forgotten her panic over her mother's health by now. The most important thing about the letter was that it made the date of their departure definite. Home in a week; she balanced the thought in her mind and wondered whether she was more pleased or sorry. It would be lovely to see her parents again; but this was Sarah country. Somehow she didn't think the dreams would carry on at home, so she would never know what had happened to Sarah. Or perhaps there was nothing to know. If Uncle Clement was right, Sarah had never been a real person.

But even if she hadn't she was real now. Real enough for the others to want to hear the rest of the story; and real enough for Polly to want to know herself. She could put up with the dreams to find out, although they were nasty while they were actually happening.

She wandered round the house and saw the dream world spread about her. The kitchen was Mrs. Piper's territory. Her uncle and aunt's big front bedroom was Uncle Simon's; her own, of course, was Sarah's.

Aunt Sylvia came upon her standing in the middle of Uncle Clement's den, trying with half-closed eyes to recapture the dread atmosphere of Mr. Stampenstone's study.

"What *are* you doing, dear? I'd rather you children didn't play in here, if you don't mind."

"I was just . . ." murmured Polly, blushing slightly. "I won't come in again."

They went out for a walk and she related the next installment of the story. When she went to tuck Hugh into bed that evening she asked in surprise: "Where's Number Three?"

Hugh pointed, thumb in mouth. The bear was sitting on the sill outside the closed window.

"What on earth's he doing there? Poor Number Three, he might fall off."

"He's Uncle Simon," said Hugh sternly. "He's got to spend the night out there as a punishment for being so nasty."

"Oh," said Polly, and went down to dinner.

They were halfway through the second course when

she thought she heard crying. "Is that Hugh?" she wondered aloud.

"Is what Hugh?"

"Someone's crying."

"Perhaps you'd better go and see what's wrong," sighed her aunt. After Polly had gone she listened herself and remarked: "I can't hear anything."

"Nor can I," said Uncle Clement. "Oh dear, I hope Polly's not starting up that nonsense again."

"Which nonsense?"

"She's determined to find ghosts in this house. She's already heard mysterious crying once, if you remember."

"Oh yes," said Aunt Sylvia vaguely.

"The trouble is she doesn't know where imagination stops and reality begins."

The mournful crying ceased just as Polly reached the landing. She stopped dead, reminded at once of the last occasion when this had happened. She felt suddenly brisk and determined; this time she would pin the thing down and none of the facts would escape her.

She peeped into the boys' room and found Hugh snugly curled up with his bear. "Poor Number Three," he was crooning. "There there. You needn't be Uncle Simon any more." It was no good mentioning crying to him; he would probably say it had been Number Three complaining about his exile. Michael's bed was empty, and she found him sitting on the end of Jennifer's in the next room.

"Did either of you hear anything just now?"

"Only you coming upstairs," said Jennifer.

"Why?" asked Michael, suddenly alert and anxious.

"Aunt Sylvia thought the cat knocked something over. Don't talk too long, you two. Good night."

Just to be sure, she tried the other two bedrooms on this floor and then went up to her own. They were all empty. She had expected them to be. She finished up with a token glance from her window, though she was quite certain the crying had been inside the house.

She lingered a moment, leaning on the sill. The lawn was completely in shadow. She could see the place where she had been standing when she heard it the other time. She remembered how she had looked up at Frederick's closed window—he really did like to stifle. Her own, just above, had been open. The sound could really have come through that more easily.

Her wandering thoughts gathered and hit her. The crying could have been in this room. She held on to the sill. How quiet it was up here; and how very, very cold.

A board creaked behind her. Her heart jumped and her hands were suddenly slippery. For a moment she was quite unable to turn round; then she forced herself. The room was empty, but her nerve had gone. She galloped down the uncarpeted stairs, along the landing, down the wider flight to the hall, and entered the dining room panting.

"Must you be so headlong, dear?" Aunt Sylvia sounded pained.

Polly burst into speech, forgetting how calm she had meant to be.

"It's happened again! It stopped when I got up there, and it wasn't any of the children, and I looked in all the other rooms—there's nobody else up there at all!"

"What do you mean, nobody else up there?" Her aunt looked quite annoyed. "Of course there isn't; it was unnecessary to conduct a search."

"They hadn't heard anything," Polly rushed on. "It must be that you can only hear it downstairs."

"That who can?" asked Uncle Clement calmly.

"Well—people," said Polly, staring.

"You're the only one who heard it, you know."

"Me? . . . No," said Polly. She looked slowly at them all, and pleaded to her aunt: "You heard it, didn't you? You said to go and see what it was."

"No, dear, I must confess I didn't hear a thing."

"Well . . . oh, I don't like it," exclaimed Polly tremulously. "I wish it would stop happening."

"Now, Polly, control yourself," said Uncle Clement, kind but firm. "Nothing at all has happened, except that you've let your imagination run away with you as usual."

The dislike she felt for him had a stiffening effect on Polly. She pushed down her fright and became sulky and defiant instead. "No I haven't."

"And did you say you'd been telling this to the younger ones?" he asked in sharper tones.

"No, I just asked if they'd heard anything. I didn't say why."

"I don't want you frightening them."

"Don't worry," she said rather pertly. "I won't."

"Polly, are you going to eat that? We're all waiting for you, you know." Her aunt's voice chilled her, and she took up her spoon in silence.

While Polly had been upstairs Frederick had thought it would be a very good thing if his father took a firm line with her nonsense; but while it was actually happening it made him uneasy. He didn't like to see her later, sitting alone in the dining room doing nothing. He went in.

"Would you like to play chess?"

"I don't know how," said Polly. Then: "Fluff, didn't you hear anything? Not even faintly?"

"No, I'm afraid I didn't." He rubbed his nose in embarrassment.

"I suppose you think I made it up, too," she said dejectedly.

"You can't blame Dad if he does think that," evaded Frederick.

"I don't tell lies!" flashed Polly.

"Well . . . Polly . . . what about Captain, for instance?"

"But that was absolutely different," she protested. "I never thought Captain was real."

"Maybe you didn't, but the younger ones did."

"Yes," said Polly, remembering. "I never quite realized how much they believed in him until Michael asked me point-blank."

"What did you say?"

"I had to say I'd made him up, of course. He was disappointed. But anyway," she went on impatiently, "that was just a game. Can't you see how it was different?"

"I can see how it looks the same to Dad."

"But I haven't said anything about it to the little ones."

"No, this time it's us you want to convince."

"All right then, don't believe me." She tried to sound

cold, but the childish tremble was in her voice again.

"Oh, let's not talk about it. Come and learn chess. I think you might be good at it."

She went, because there was nothing else to do. Frederick was a good teacher and she picked the rules up quickly. She began to enjoy herself, and forgot about the crying until it was time to go to bed.

She had been careful to say nothing about the panic that had sent her rushing downstairs; after all, it had had no concrete cause. She didn't suppose, when she thought about it afterwards, that the crying was more likely to have come from her bedroom than any other part of the house. She had simply had a delayed reaction to hearing it again, and being on her own right up here had made it worse—so she told herself, but she undressed very quickly, with frequent glances over her shoulder.

Once in bed she felt safe. Now she could relax and think about Sarah, particularly about the last dream; that, she hoped, would put her in the right mood for dreaming some more. She must make the most of her remaining nights here. (She wondered fleetingly if going to bed would be terribly dull when she got home.)

She went to sleep quickly, and slipped successfully into the kitchen of the other world.

Sarah was gently closing the oven door on a tray of pale buns.

"Not the right color yet," she reported.

"Pity," said Mrs. Piper. "We could've 'ad one with our tea. Sit down and drink yours now, before it gets cold."

Sarah obeyed, trying not to let her eyes slide towards the kitchen door. Uncle Simon didn't know about their midmorning break; and although Mrs. Piper comfortably assured her that if he ever found out and tried to stop it she'd fix him, Sarah could never relax completely.

"I'm glad he said I was to learn to cook. I like it," she said.

"Well, I dare say there'll be times in your life when you'll be glad to know 'ow. I don't know what 'e was thinking of, though. You don't need cooking to be a 'ousemaid, and I don't s'pose anyone'd take on a little thing like you as a general."

"Is plum cake difficult?" asked Sarah dreamily, not really paying attention.

"You'd learn it easy enough. You've picked up the rest right quick. But 'e won't 'ave anything so rich made 'ere, so that's that. 'E likes to live plain."

"Perhaps he's really poor."

"Not 'im. Just 'is meanness." She took a drink of tea. "Now if 'e'd let you, you could come to tea at our cottage and 'ave a piece of my plum cake. I'd make one special."

"He wouldn't, though."

"Dare say not. Not worth asking. 'E been banging that 'eathen gong at you lately?"

"No, he seems to be forgetting about it. I haven't been out very much, though. It's too cold."

"Might as well be the dog," muttered Mrs. Piper, still indignant.

A bell rang in the kitchen.

" 'E would. Soon as I get off me feet," she grumbled, and went out to the study. Sarah had another look at her buns, decided they were done, and took them out of the oven. Then she rinsed their teacups, dried them, and put them away. Mrs. Piper was still gone, and she thought she heard raised voices coming from the study. She wondered what they were talking about.

When Mrs. Piper returned she was red-faced and breathing hard. She sat down heavily at the table and looked at nothing.

"Well," she said. "That's that."

"What?" asked Sarah.

"A week's notice, that's what. After all these years." Sarah gazed, blank with astonishment. Mrs. Piper continued: "Not that I care for meself. Jack's been wanting me to give up for a long while; find something else. Oh, I told 'im straight—'*im* I mean, not Jack—I said to 'im, I said, 'I'd never 'ave stayed on if it 'adn't been for your poor mother's sake.' She was a good lady; she did a lot of good in the village. '*I* don't care,' I said, 'but it's not fair to Sarah. It's 'ard enough for a grown woman to do the work of this 'ouse—' "

"What do you mean?" whispered Sarah.

Mrs. Piper recalled her eyes from the distance and fixed them on Sarah's face. "Eh, it's not right," she grunted. "You poor love."

"Am I to work here? Instead of you? Instead of going away?"

"That's 'ow it seems. The mean old devil's seen a way to save my wages."

"He said he couldn't afford my keep."

"You'll be worth more than your keep," said Mrs. Piper bluntly. "No wonder 'e wanted me to teach you cooking."

"Oh dear." All Sarah's desolation was in her voice.

"Did we drink all that tea?" Mrs. Piper was on her feet and bustling round again. "No, there's a good bit left in the pot. Where's your cup?"

"I washed them."

"I'll wash 'em again after. There, now you drink that up. Nothing like a cup of tea when you're low."

Sarah drank, breaking off with a start when the bell rang.

"Drat that wretched thing! I've a good mind to smash it before I go." Mrs. Piper went out, returning in a moment to say: "It's you 'e wants now."

"Ah, Sarah," said her uncle. "Come in and shut the door." He was standing on the hearthrug. "Has Mrs. Piper explained to you what your new duties will be?"

"Yes, sir," she replied expressionlessly.

"Perhaps I should say your new responsibilities. I hope you realize I am placing a great deal of faith in you, a girl of your age."

Sarah opened her mouth to say she wished he wouldn't, but realized in time that she would only be accused of ingratitude.

"Well, Sarah? Don't stand there looking like a gold-fish." An irritable look replaced his smile. "I hope I'm not going to be disappointed in you."

"So do I, sir."

"Are you being impertinent, girl?"

"No, sir," said Sarah hurriedly. "I'll do my best, sir."

"Very well, you may go."

"Don't you let 'im wear you out, dear," said Mrs. Piper on her last morning, a week later. "If the work starts piling up, you tell 'im you need 'elp; 'e'll 'ave to get me back one or two days a week."

"I shall have the afternoons, too. I think I shall be able to manage." She wasn't afraid of the work. It was being here alone with him that she dreaded, forever and ever with no escape.

"Remember I'm only in the village, not so very far away."

No; but in forbidden country.

"I shall come back to see you, mind. 'E can't stop me doing that. We'll 'ave a cup of tea in the kitchen, just like now."

Sarah quickly picked up her cup and took a sip to hide the trembling of her lips.

"And you be sure and see you 'ave your break each morning. Don't go doing without just 'cause I'm not 'ere to make the tea."

"I won't," promised Sarah.

She got up at five o'clock next day. She didn't know how long it would take her to do everything on her own, and she was terrified of not having breakfast ready on time.

The kitchen was cheerless and black, and for a moment she longed for the sound of Mrs. Piper's key in the back door. Then she lit the lamp and attacked the cold stove, and was soon too busy to think.

Later on, when the fires were beginning to burn brightly and a rosy-pale dawn showed a thick coating of frost on everything outside, she felt almost happy. She was getting on well, time was on her side; she hummed a little song as she moved around the kitchen.

Then she heard a tiny sound from outside the back door. She stood still and listened. There it was again, a thin high-pitched mew. She opened the door and found a kitten scurrying off on wobbly legs. She called to it softly and it crouched a few yards away, a shivering scrap of gray fur with big frightened eyes.

"Puss," she murmured, and held out one hand. "Puss, puss, puss."

It mewed again, a desperate bleat of hunger. Frost crunched beneath her feet as she went towards it; then she picked it up. She could feel its ribs, and a heart thudding fit to shake them apart.

There was a scraping sound and Thugdon's head came out of his kennel, his breath steaming in the cold air. The kitten hissed and went rigid; trying to twist out of her arms it scratched her hand. Its tail stuck up under her nose, looking like a bottle brush.

"Hello, Thugdon, it's all right," said Sarah, and took the kitten into the kitchen. It backed into a corner when she put it down, but came out to the saucer of milk she placed a foot or two away; dipped a nose in, sneezed, and then began to lap furiously. She was relieved that it knew how. By the time she had found a bit of Thugdon's meat the saucer was empty. She refilled it with meat and bread, cut up small. The kitten knew how to eat also. Its tail had returned to normal size and lay out along the floor; its haunches stuck up sharply through its fur.

When the saucer was empty again it circled the kitchen twice and jumped lightly on to the only chair with a cushion.

"You've been in houses before," decided Sarah.

It aimed a few vague licks at itself with a pale rasping tongue; then curled round and closed its eyes. Sarah washed the saucer, wiped the crumbs off the floor, and wondered what to do. It might once have had a home, but it must have been some time ago; it was nothing but fur and bones now, weighing less than a feather. She wondered if her uncle would let her inquire in the village whether anyone had lost a kitten; but then suppose nobody had?

It seemed to be asleep. Its sides moved regularly and rapidly in and out; but presently a little crackling sound began to come with each outward breath. Once, twice, a dozen times, and finally it became a continuous purr. It was rather uneven, as though the kitten hadn't had much practice yet.

Sarah saw what she must do. She went to the foot of the stairs and listened; all was quiet above. Back to the kitchen; it was a shame to disturb the kitten's rest, but it couldn't be helped. Cradling it against her chest she crept up the stairs, along the landing, past her uncle's room (praying that it wouldn't made any sound) on up the attic stairs into her room. It wasn't as warm as the kitchen, and the kitten prowled restlessly for a little while; but it was very tired, and settled down eventually on her bed. "Goodbye for now, little gray one," she whispered.

As she closed the heavy door and tiptoed down the stairs she realized the enormity of her action. She was committed now; committed to keeping a secret pet. But when she saw the clock she stopped thinking about the kitten. She had spent far longer on it than she realized, and time was no longer on her side; she would have to work as fast as possible now.

Frantic efforts got breakfast to the table in time, but left Sarah hot and untidy and still in her apron. She realized this too late, just as she was carrying the plate in. Her uncle sat looking her coolly up and down for a long moment; then asked:

"Have you by any chance glanced in a mirror lately, Sarah?"

"I've been so busy, sir," she apologized awkwardly.

"So you spared yourself the sight?" He smiled thinly. "Well, you can spare me also. If you're going to look like a servant I really think it would be better if you ate in the kitchen."

"Yes, sir." Scarlet with humiliation, Sarah took up her plate.

"I'll ring when I've finished."

She sat down at the kitchen table and wondered if this was to be a permanent arrangement. On the whole she hoped it was; the less time she spent in his company the happier she would be. And there was nobody to witness her degradation—she didn't even feel very degraded, once away from his stinging tongue. In herself she felt more like a servant than a niece.

Halfway through the morning she risked a visit to her bedroom. The kitten was strolling up and down the window sill, but when she came in it took a flying leap and landed, light as thistledown, in front of her.

"Hello, gray one," she murmured.

It wound in and out of her feet, brushing her with a hopefully vertical tail, and mewed. She was glad her room was away up here and had a thick door.

"I'm sorry," she said. "I haven't any food. I didn't think you'd be hungry again so soon."

She noticed a dark stain on the boards in one corner. "Oh, gray one . . . I suppose you couldn't help it." She was lucky it had been no more. It presented a problem, though. A box of earth; wasn't that what people used? There was an empty wooden box in the kitchen, and she decided she had better fill it at once. It proved unexpectedly difficult; the frosty ground was as hard as iron and a shovel, the only implement she could find, made no impression on it whatever. Then she thought of ashes. That was easy; a few shovelfuls were quite sufficient. From the kitchen she took a length or two of bacon rind and set off upstairs, trembling a little as she bore her outlandish burden past the study door.

The kitten gobbled the rind but showed no interest in the box, which she placed firmly in the corner where the stain had been. She hoped it would understand her wishes next time it had an errand in that direction. When she bent down to stroke it she was rewarded by a brief burst of purring and more sinuous rubbings round her ankles. She was loath to leave it, but she didn't dare stay any longer.

"Don't make too much noise now," she admonished. "Goodbye."

9 ♛ *Filling the Lake*

"Go on," said Michael.

"Not now," said Polly. "That's all for today."

"When will you go on? Tomorrow?"

"Maybe."

"I'm glad she found that kitten," said Hugh.

"Yes, but what if her uncle discovers it!" Jennifer shuddered.

"Do please go on a bit, we're so worried about him discovering it," begged Michael.

"No. Don't pester."

The younger ones got up and went away dissatisfied, leaving Polly and Frederick in possession of the fallen tree trunk where they had all been sitting.

"I hope you won't make her uncle too nasty to be true," he remarked.

"You don't have to go on listening," said Polly coolly, knowing that he would; he was quite as interested in Sarah's story as the others. "Besides, *I* don't make him anything."

"Is it still based on dreams, then?"

"It is dreams." Frederick received this in silence. "I suppose you don't believe me."

He didn't want to start a quarrel. He said carefully "I think you tell them well."

"Thanks," said Polly, who didn't really want to quarrel either; the day was too warm. "Let's walk farther along."

She sprang off the tree trunk. The lake was between them and the house; they hadn't explored down here before. When they caught up with the others they were standing in a dry ditch.

"Look, a funny kind of gully," said Michael. "I wonder who made it."

"Nobody made it," said Frederick. "It's the bed of a stream. The same stream as higher up."

"How can it be? That runs into the lake."

"Well, this comes from the lake."

Michael walked up the little valley and reached the edge of the lake in a few moments.

"When the water level's high enough it runs away down here," said Frederick. "It acts as an overflow."

"I should like to see it running," said Polly. "If we just dug it a bit deeper it would. Let's try it."

"That would lower the whole lake, and it's low enough already," said Frederick. "Mother doesn't like it low; the mud at the edges smells."

Polly sniffed hard. "It's a lovely seaside smell."

"Rather like rotting seaweed," agreed Frederick drily.

"Let's pretend it is the sea, and paddle," said Jennifer.

"Don't be silly, it's too deep, and you know we're

not allowed to play in it. Come away from the edge," ordered Polly.

"We're nowhere near the edge," they complained, moving back a little.

"Dry streams are sad," said Polly thoughtfully. "It ought to run. I don't see why it doesn't. There's all that water coming into the lake, where does it go?"

"All what water?" said Frederick. "A mere trickle."

"But the stream's quite strong where it comes in through the top wall, up by the pool," said Michael.

"I suppose most of it soaks away into the ground," replied Frederick indifferently.

"If we could stop it doing that . . ." mused Polly. "The stream's pretty jammed up in places. Let's go and clear all the muck out of it so it can all run into the lake, and then this one'll run, too. We'll get a current right across the lake; we could float boats across—it's all right, it wouldn't be playing in the lake," she added hastily, seeing Frederick's mouth open. "We could start them in the stream."

"Yes, come on," said Michael excitedly. "Let's begin now." They rushed off around the lake.

"You'll each need a good strong stick," Polly called after them, and began to look round for one for herself. "Are you going to help, Fluff?"

"I suppose I might as well," he said in lordly tones.

Polly picked up a large branch. "I could break the twigs off," she mused.

"It looks rotten to me. Here's one that's healthy," grunted Frederick, trying and failing to break the stick he held. "Straight, too. Here."

"Gosh, thanks, but what about you?"

"I'll find another. Here's a good one."

They strode off, picking remnants of loose bark from their equipment.

"We'll begin at the bottom where it comes under the drive, and work our way up," decided Polly.

"If we began at the top we'd have extra water helping us when we got here," said Frederick, looking distastefully at the black sludge choking the mouth of the stream.

"No, we ought to do the nasty part first. Then when we come down here again we'll find it transformed."

The younger ones were excited by this picture and made an instant start. Frederick, convinced almost at once that he could do it better, began to help. Once down at water level he saw with relief that even Polly couldn't expect them to clean out the tunnel under the drive; the arch was too low to admit anyone.

It was hot work. Frederick soon shed his sweater and tie, hanging them neatly over the branch of a tree. His cousins, who were wearing nothing but open-necked shirts and cotton dresses respectively, anyway, couldn't follow suit; but a few minutes later Michael looked sideways at Polly and began to unbutton his shirt.

"Put it on a tree, then," she said.

Frederick was astonished at the satisfaction to be had from removing a dam and releasing a scummy, eddying pocket of water in one joyful swirl. Occasional spongy ground on either side of the stream showed where the water which didn't reach the lake had been going.

"Hugh isn't helping," said Jennifer.

"It makes my feet wet," said Hugh gloomily. "I don't like this game much."

"Go down to the drive and you can watch the water coming more and more," suggested Polly. Hugh squelched away, trailing his stick.

"My feet are wet, too," said Michael.

"So are mine. Let's take our shoes and socks off," said Jennifer.

Polly and Frederick, who had taken care to keep their own feet relatively dry, and who realized how sharp the rocks would be to bare soles, advised them not to; but they were determined. Frederick did wonder about going back to the house and changing into hip boots, but decided he couldn't be bothered.

Polly was too busy to remember that they must be approaching the pool until suddenly the sound of the waterfall rose above the noise they were making themselves.

"Good, that means we've just about finished." Frederick straightened his aching back.

Polly seized on this. "Yes, we have, haven't we. Come on then, back to the lake!"

Nobody moved. "But, Polly," began Jennifer indignantly.

"We must go right to the very top," insisted Michael.

"It'll mean passing the pool," said Polly gravely.

"They don't mind the pool," broke in Frederick, irritated.

"What do you know about it?" demanded Polly.

"They didn't mind it a bit when they came here with me."

"No, we didn't," agreed Jennifer. "We like it."

"You never told me you'd come here again." Polly felt oddly betrayed.

"We forgot." Michael took her hand and gazed at her earnestly. "You see, Polly, there was nothing here really. It was just we got frightened like people do in woods."

It was bad enough that she already felt the first creepings of panic along her spine; to have Michael explaining her fear to her was too much. She shook him off and exclaimed fiercely: "All right then, we'll go to the very top; and since we're removing dams, what about that one there?" She pointed to the fall.

After a pause Frederick said: "It would take us ages."

"But think how the water would rush down," said Michael.

"It would be a tidal wave," said Polly. "It would swoosh down the stream scouring everything we've missed away."

"If we weakened it gradually from this side . . ." pondered Frederick, "it would eventually give way all at once."

"Come on!" exclaimed Jennifer, splashing in among the spray.

"No, careful, careful—keep to the bank," said Frederick. "You don't want the whole lot coming down on top of you."

Under his directions they attacked the dam, heaving at slippery green boulders and dumping them on the bank, carefully levering out the larger ones which took two people to lift. In spite of their care Frederick crushed a finger and Polly got a shoeful of water; but they labored on. They were possessed by the excitement of destruction. At last came the grand moment when the rocks began to rumble and slip independently. Leaping aside with yells of triumph they saw the whole dam collapse in a thunder of escaping water.

"Keep up with it!" cried Polly; and they rushed down the bank in the wake of the lolloping wave. It smoothed out as it went, but even so the lower part of the stream was running far more strongly than ever before. When they reached the drive they rested, listening admiringly to the new sounds they had created: the deep musical echo from the tunnel, and the steady plashing where the stream spilled into the lake.

"I think the level's a bit higher already," said Frederick.

"Oh quick!" exclaimed Polly. "I want to see it start overflowing."

They charged around the lake to the dry ditch. It was dry still, but the water was definitely nearer its mouth.

"It won't take long," said Polly confidently.

"Couldn't we help it a little?"

"No, we must let it happen all by itself." She forgot she had previously urged the opposite.

Actually the water rose very slowly indeed, and the younger ones got bored and went away. Frederick wasn't held by the same fascination as Polly, but he stayed because he had no energy to move. At last she called to the others.

"It's gotten there! Do you want to see?"

They came running, but the sight was disappointing: a thin dusty trickle which quickly lost itself among the dead leaves. Frederick worried for a moment that Polly would suggest clearing the channel now; however, she too was tired.

"Oh well, it's happened," she said. "We'll come back after supper. It'll be running better then."

When they went into the house they found they had been gone longer than they thought; in fact Uncle Clement was home.

"Good heavens," said Aunt Sylvia blankly, "what have you been doing? And where are all your clothes? You're absolutely filthy, every one of you."

"We've been playing in the stream," said Polly.

"Our things are in the wood; it's all right, we know where we left them," said Frederick. As they departed to retrieve them Polly heard Uncle Clement say, "Frederick has discovered the charms of the Great Outdoors," and Aunt Sylvia reply without enthusiasm, "It's not a bit like him."

Aunt Sylvia insisted on a bath for each of the younger ones; Frederick and Polly were told to have a thorough wash. Uncle Clement was intrigued to know what had kept them out so long. They explained, and he said he must go and inspect their handiwork later. But when Michael blurted out that the big dam had gone too, his benevolent look faded a little, and he and Aunt Sylvia questioned Frederick disapprovingly.

Frederick felt their displeasure was quite justified; his only excuse was that he had been carried away by the joys of undamming. The only one who was neither sorry nor ashamed was Polly. Whatever anyone said, she had hated the pool and was glad it was gone.

She went to bed early, saying she felt tired. Actually she was impatient for the next dream. Although she had been short with the others, she was anxious about the kitten herself; so anxious, it turned out, that she couldn't sleep. She lay chewing her nails in annoyance and frustration, and was still wide awake when she heard Frederick come up to bed.

She tried to be sensible. She was bound to get to sleep eventually, and the less she fretted the sooner it would be. But suppose even then she didn't dream? An awful thought; she mustn't waste a night when there were so few left. She simply had to know what happened to Sarah. And what would the others say if the story broke off in the middle?

Only it would have to, sooner or later. She groaned softly at the realization: she couldn't dream Sarah's whole life. When it came to the last dream, she would have to tell it so that it seemed like a proper ending. But would it be a happy one?

She began to think about the stream and imagined herself busy again, moving blockage after blockage. It was rather like counting sheep. . . .

The next thing she was aware of was Sarah's room, with Gray One chasing a ball of paper round the floor. It moved easily when he batted it, and he pursued it excitedly, slipping and slithering. Sarah laughed as she watched.

Her uncle had a visitor downstairs: his doctor. He had told Sarah at lunch that he would be coming, and she had asked if she should bring them tea. He had said no; "and I shall let him in myself. There'll be no need for you to be downstairs at all." This seemed rather like a veiled command to stay out of the way; so after hurrying through her tasks in the kitchen she had come up here to enjoy her unexpected free time with Gray One.

He looked very different now from the stray he had been. His sides had filled out and his fur was silky-soft. He was a substantial handful to lift; and on the bed at night Sarah could feel his warm weight tightening the blankets in the crook of her knees.

She could never open the window more than a crack for fear he would get out on the roof. He haunted the sill, as though he wanted to be as near as possible to the outside world. Sometimes he lay on it and basked in the spring sunshine; but when he paced up and down swinging his tail and uttering little melancholy cries as he watched the birds, she felt worried about the life of imprisonment he was forced to lead.

He ate mostly scraps; it didn't seem fair to Thugdon to steal too much of his meat. By careful maneuvers (chiefly going without herself) she managed to save quite a lot of milk for Gray One, and mixed it with water to make it go further.

He had made use of his box right from the start. Sarah changed the ashes every few days, but it was a job she dreaded; if her uncle caught her with the box it could never be explained away.

She never wondered if Gray One was worth the trouble. He stopped her feeling lonely; all her spare time (not that she had much now) was spent up here, and whenever she came into the room he rushed to jump into her arms, purring like a little machine. She was fond of Thugdon, but he didn't belong to her. She loved Gray One.

She looked at the clock, and wondered how much longer the doctor would stay. She didn't know whether the visit was medical or friendly; her uncle didn't seem to be ill, except for the way she had seen him once or twice holding his chest after climbing the stairs, as though he had stitch.

Like an echo of her thoughts, she caught the alarming sound of footsteps ascending from below. She sat frozen, ears straining. They would stop at the first floor; they must. Her uncle never came up here.

The steps came on. She looked frantically around the room; then grabbed Gray One and put him under the bed.

"Stay there!" she hissed, making a dive for the ash-box and thrusting that too into the dimness. His eyes shone indignantly at her, but his crouching form remained still. The ball of paper and an empty saucer joined him just as her uncle opened the door.

"You're to come downstairs," he said abruptly; then sniffed, wrinkling his nose in disgust. "This room smells. Don't you ever give it an airing?"

Sarah gulped and began to blush. She knew he was right; how could it help getting stuffy, with Gray One cooped up here all the while?

"Open the window for heaven's sake, and give me that chair. I need a rest after all those stairs."

She rushed to obey, tripping over her feet in her anxiety. He seated himself and announced:

"Dr. Lawson wants to see you."

"Wants to see me?" She could not suppress her astonishment that someone should penetrate her narrow world.

"Try not to look like an idiot," he exclaimed irritably. "He won't eat you. He just wants to pay his respects to—" his face twisted—"my niece. All you're required to do is answer when he addresses you. Understand?"

"Y—yes."

He frowned. "Well, you can't come down like that. Brush your hair and put on something respectable."

"My—my Sunday dress, sir?"

"Is it all you have? Then I suppose it must serve. Be quick about it."

He stood up rather slowly, with a cautious expression she had never seen him wear before. If it was a medical visit, she didn't think the doctor could have been reassuring.

Gray One chose that moment to emerge from hiding and make for the open window. Uncle Simon's jaw fell open.

"What—" he said, his face darkening. "What the deuce—"

Sarah couldn't speak. Her hands clasped each other desperately and wrapped themselves in her pinafore. The kitten sprang on to the sill, and her uncle took a threatening step towards him.

Panic loosened her tongue. "Oh please!" she cried. "Please don't hurt him, he's mine, please please—"

He gripped her shoulder. "Stop that caterwauling," he rasped. "Stop it at once, do you hear?"

She stopped.

"So it's yours, is it? How long have you had it? What does it eat?"

"S—s—scraps . . ."

His hand was digging into her bones. He seemed to

be leaning half his weight on her. "My food," he breathed. "You deceitful little minx—no wonder the room smells like a pigsty."

His face changed. He released her and sat heavily on the bed. One hand went to his chest, and the look of caution was back.

"I shan't discuss this now," he said after a moment. "Change your dress. Follow me down."

He got up and went out.

Sarah was shaking all over. She had lost all desire to see the doctor, but she knew she must obey her uncle. She closed the window first of all; she couldn't let Gray One risk falling off the roof when he had just escaped being hurled to the ground by her uncle—she was sure that intention had been in his mind, even if only for a second.

In the study she found Uncle Simon reclining in an armchair with Dr. Lawson standing over him.

"Now mind what I say and treat stairs with respect." He broke off as Sarah entered the room and turned to her with a slow smile. He had a ginger moustache and friendly blue eyes.

"Well well. So this is Margaret's little girl."

Sarah actually felt her size diminish as she murmured shyly: "Good afternoon, sir."

He shook her hand firmly, saying: "I'm very happy to meet you, my dear. And how do you like living at Greystones?"

"I—I—like the woods." She slid a nervous glance towards her uncle, wondering if she had said the right thing.

"And now the winter's over you must get outside

and enjoy them. Run around and put some roses in your cheeks." said the doctor cheerfully.

"Sarah is pale by nature," observed her uncle. "She plays outside a great deal."

"Yes," said Sarah, though lately it hadn't been true.

"You must find it rather lonely here."

"Sarah likes to read."

"Well well." The doctor regarded her quizzically for a few minutes. "You're lucky to have inherited your mother's looks."

Sarah's mind's eye saw her mother's dear remembered face, which had never seemed much to resemble the single old photograph she kept of a pretty laughing girl. A confusion of emotions made her cheeks grow warm.

"Ah, now you've got a bit of color!" said the doctor delightedly. "I think it's the black dress that makes you look so pale. Need you still wear mourning, my dear? I confess I don't like to see children in black."

Sarah didn't know what to say. This, before it was dyed, had been her best dress when her mother was alive; her other clothes were few and very shabby.

"Sarah wishes to show proper respect for the dead," said her uncle repressively.

She gazed down at her lap, relieved to be saved the necessity of a reply.

"Yes, yes, of course." Dr. Lawson sounded apologetic, and changed the subject quickly. "By the way, if anything should by an unlucky chance happen to you, Sarah is provided for, of course?"

"Sarah, will you fetch us some tea."

The doctor looked rather surprised at the interruption. As Sarah hurried out her uncle began: "Alas, these are hard times, and my literary activities bring in barely enough on which to manage. . . ."

As soon as she reached the kitchen Sarah's mind switched to the awful problem of Gray One. Her hands prepared tea automatically while she speculated fearfully on what punishments he would receive. She hoped the doctor wouldn't leave for a long while.

When she wheeled the trolley into the study he was saying "But the house?"

Uncle Simon shook his head. "Mortgaged." He looked the tea things over and said in tones of controlled annoyance, "You've forgotten to bring china for yourself. Do you intend to starve?"

Sarah gazed blankly for a moment. It was weeks since she had last shared a meal with him. But of course, a visitor's being here must make it different.

The doctor made kind and determined conversation to her while they ate, and she tried to answer sensibly and ignore the smouldering silence into which her uncle had fallen. She was sure he was thinking about Gray One.

Eventually the doctor rose to take his leave. Sarah stayed in the study while they went to the front door. When her uncle returned she faced him stiffly, hands behind her back so that he shouldn't see them trembling.

"Take the tea away." That was all he said; he sat down and gazed broodingly into the fire.

This was a new kind of punishment: the torture of suspense. He was cold and withdrawn for the rest of the day, and had still said nothing when Sarah went to bed. She couldn't sleep; she lay stroking Gray One until her hand ached, unable to believe he would still be here tomorrow night.

Suddenly the bed was more comfortable, and the kitten no longer purred beside her. . . . She was Polly, she was waking up.

I won't, I'm not awake, I won't open my eyes. The dream mustn't stop, I can't let it. I've got to know about Gray One. I'm Sarah, I'm Sarah asleep.

But there was a jump, and instead she was Sarah in the morning. She set Uncle Simon's breakfast before him and was just going out when he raised his head and looked at her sharply.

"By the way, Sarah. That animal."

She tried to control the start she gave.

"Get rid of it."

"N—now, sir?"

"After breakfast. Take it and lose it somewhere, and it'd better not be near enough for it to find its way back here. I shall wring the wretched creature's neck if I see it again."

Now she knew the worst her knees turned to jelly. She crept out of the room without a word. It would be useless to plead. All the same, she wouldn't obey him to the letter. She must find another home for Gray One; she couldn't possibly abandon him.

It was a sunny day, almost warm. A mist of tiny green leaves covered the hawthorns by the lane, and there were daisies and dandelions growing in the grass verge. She would have enjoyed her walk to the village if it hadn't been for the burden she carried.

Gray One must be terribly cramped inside the sack, but she hadn't had anything else to carry him in. She knew he wouldn't stay in her arms for long, and she doubted he'd accompany her on foot as Thugdon would have done. Sometimes he was quiet; but every so often he began to struggle again, uttering frantic cries. Talking to him seemed to soothe him a little.

When she knocked at the first of the cottages she had a speech all ready for the woman who answered the door.

"I'm sorry to bother you, but did you lose a gray kitten two or three months ago?"

A blank stare and a shaking head.

"Well, would you like one? I can't k—keep him any longer, you see. . . ."

The head went on shaking. "No thank you." The door closed.

It was the same everywhere. Nobody had lost a kitten; nobody wanted one.

"Looks more like a cat to me," said one woman darkly. Gray One was struggling at the time, and the sack appeared full of legs. "Have kittens itself pretty soon, I shouldn't wonder."

"He's not full-grown, and he really is a tom," said Sarah earnestly. "Would you like to look?"

"And get my face scratched? No thank you."

Another time it was: "I dare say that the people who lost him did it on purpose. They won't want him back. People with cats get more than enough kittens."

In her preoccupation it was a wonderful surprise when at last a door was opened by a familiar face.

"Oh, Mrs. Piper!" she said.

"Why, 'o'd 'ave thought it?" came the delighted reply. "You've managed to come and see me! Eh, come on in and let's 'ave a proper look at you. 'Ow are you then? Not so bad? I'm sorry I've never come up like I said; I feel right bad about it, but Jack's been poorly. . . ."

"Oh, I'm sorry." Sarah managed to squeeze this in.

"Well, 'e's getting better now. Why, whatever in the world 'ave you got there?"

"It's—it's my kitten," gulped Sarah, suddenly finding it needed a great effort not to cry. She began to explain.

"No, 'e'd never let you keep a pet,' nodded Mrs. Piper at the end. 'Eh, what a shame. And you've been trying to find puss a home? Well, you needn't look any farther."

Sarah faltered. "Would you really . . ."

"Course I would, dear. Let 'im out now and I'll give 'im a drink."

Gray One shot out of the sack with ruffled fur and a wild look in his eyes. He allowed Sarah to pick him up, but he spat at Mrs. Piper when she tried to stroke him, and would only drink the milk after considerable coaxing by Sarah.

" 'E's feeling strange. It's only natural. We'll 'ave to keep the door shut for the first few days, until 'e's used to us, to stop 'im wandering back."

Sarah tried to slip away unnoticed while Gray One drank, but he rushed across the room when the door opened. She had to shut it in his face. Of course he mustn't be allowed to wander back, not after what her uncle had said . . . but the sound of his desperate claws against the wood haunted her as she walked slowly home.

She could hardly believe her eyes when she opened the back door. Uncle Simon was sitting by the kitchen table, sprawling on the chair with his chin resting on his chest.

"Shut the door," he rasped without moving.

His legs were sticking out, prominently displaying damp trouser-ends and muddy shoes.

"Stop staring."

"I'm sorry, sir," said Sarah mechanically, and added: "Are—are you ill?"

"Mind your own business, and give me a hand off this chair."

He dragged himself up with her help, and stood leaning partly on her and partly on the table.

"Help me upstairs."

She wondered what was wrong with him, and thought how quickly it had gotten worse. Yesterday he had merely looked frightened; now his face was pinched and gray, and he walked like an old man. And he was so heavy. She thought they would never reach the top of the stairs. Once she slipped under the weight, and he stumbled and cursed her.

"Are you trying to murder me?" he snarled breathlessly. "You're a fool if you do . . . because if I die . . . you'll have nothing."

They reached his room and he lowered himself on to the bed with a gasping laugh. "Nothing," he repeated. "Nothing . . . nothing. . . ."

Sarah wished he wouldn't behave so oddly. She didn't

dare suggest calling the doctor; he told her to go away, and she went.

There was Gray One's box in her room; she supposed she'd better throw it away. She put his ball of paper inside a drawer. She thought numbly that Uncle Simon didn't really look ill enough to die, and wondered why he'd kept saying she'd have nothing if he did. Did he expect it to upset her? But she had nothing now; she had nothing at all.

10 ❦ *Haunted Room*

Polly woke to darkness and moonlight. This time she made no effort to stay in the dream; she had had quite enough of being Sarah for one night. She almost thought she had had enough of it altogether.

She felt terribly thirsty. After enduring it for a few minutes she went down to the bathroom and drank some water out of her hands. As she emerged on to the moonlit landing she heard the crying begin.

It was just the same as before, a low desolate sobbing; only this time she was near enough to tell its exact direction. It was coming from her room.

Sarah's room. It was Sarah crying.

All the bedroom doors were closed. She thought she would wake Frederick and let him hear it for himself; but then she paused. Suppose he listened, and didn't hear anything. That would be really frightening.

She didn't feel frightened as it was; just very, very depressed. The crying was the saddest sound she had ever heard; and she knew from her own experience all the reasons for Sarah's hopeless grief.

There was no comfort she could give, but how could she ignore such misery? She cast one more glance at the closed doors. Nobody stirred behind them. Slowly she began to ascend the attic stairs.

The bedroom door must have closed itself behind her when she came down, making the blackness complete at the top of the stairs. The crying stopped just as she got there. The sudden silence was much worse than the noise. She stood still, one hand on the door handle.

In her dreams she was Sarah. Then was Sarah nothing more than Polly? If she entered the room, would she see herself?

Such an awful possibility must be settled at once. She flung open the door. There was nothing, just undrawn curtains stirring in the breeze and a square of moonlight on the floor beside her waiting bed. She scrambled in quickly and got under the covers.

She had been silly; of course Sarah wasn't her. She was a real person—no, had been a real person, and now was a real ghost.

Her heart lurched, and she began to shiver. This room was haunted. All these nights she had slept in a haunted room. No wonder she had had dreams. And what about the days, too? Her racing memory uncovered several occasions when she had felt cold or jumpy for no very good reason. Well, now she knew. What on earth had possessed her to come back up here? She must get out at once.

The floor creaked loudly.

She gave a tiny half-choked cry. She was trapped. And she couldn't call for help; who would hear her from up here, buried under the blankets as she was? But to put even her head out was unthinkable now.

She lay rigidly, clammy with the sweat of fear, her ears straining to catch further sounds. There were various little clicks and rustles that might have been anything. Her watch was on the floor, impossible to reach; but it had said three o'clock when she went down to the bathroom. How many hours until it got light? She thought at least two; how could she endure them?

But nothing happened to increase her fear, and gradually she began to relax. She made a little tunnel to let some air into her stuffy interior, and arranged her limbs more comfortably. She wished she dared put her head out on the pillow; and that was the last thought she remembered when she woke with a headache at eight o'clock.

Frederick thought Polly looked rather odd that morning. She was pasty and heavy-eyed, and picked at her breakfast with an abstracted expression. It was raining, and the younger ones were disappointed because they couldn't go out and float boats across the lake; but Polly, although it had been her idea, didn't seem to care. As the morning dragged on they became fractious and whiny. Frederick escaped to his room, but was soon hounded out again by his mother. "It looks so rude when you have guests, dear. Why don't you suggest a game of Fish?"

Heaven forbid, thought Frederick. Luckily he had

a better idea. "Tell us some more of the Sarah story."

"Oh," said Polly listlessly, "I'm not in the mood."

But eventually she was persuaded. She told it rather badly to begin with and Frederick regretted asking her. When she slipped into her usual style he wished she wouldn't charge the affair of the kitten with so much emotion. He wasn't very fond of animals himself, but he knew the younger ones were, particularly Michael. The sight of their faces made him fidget uneasily. As Polly reached the end he seized on a possible diversion.

"The Mystery of The Muddy Shoes. I wonder what he'd been doing?"

"Mmm," said Polly vaguely; she lacked the energy to tell him to wait and see.

"Poor little Gray One," said Michael.

"Poor Sarah," said Jennifer.

"Oh, Polly, why did you make him do that?" Michael burst out. "Please make him not have done it!"

"I can't," said Polly gloomily. "That's how it was."

"It didn't really happen, though, did it?" said Jennifer.

Michael, watching Polly's face, asked sharply: "Is it all true?"

"I don't think so," said Polly, but her voice lacked conviction.

"Of course it's not," exclaimed Frederick hastily.

Michael didn't even look at him. "It is," he said.

"I don't know," said Polly crossly, and stood up. "I'm going out."

"You'll get wet," said Hugh.

"I shall wear a raincoat. And I'm going by myself."

To her relief they didn't argue. She ran up to her room, pulled on her things, and managed to get out of the house without meeting Aunt Sylvia.

It was raining harder than she had thought, but she wasn't going to turn back. She had to talk to someone, and there was only one person who might believe her.

Half an hour later a disapproving Mrs. Biggs showed a bedraggled Polly into Mr. Mather's study.

"Good heavens!" he said. "You look soaked to the skin."

"I'm afraid I am rather wet," said Polly in a small voice.

"Catch her death," croaked Mrs. Biggs in the background.

"Let me see, can we dry you off at all? I'm sure you should take off your wet shoes for a start. Perhaps Mrs. Biggs can put your socks over the stove. And let's get rid of your raincoat . . . that's it . . . and then the rest of you can steam if you sit in front of the fire."

Polly removed her shoes, and parted rather more reluctantly with her socks, relieved to find her feet were clean.

"I wonder if Polly could possibly have a hot drink, Mrs. Biggs?"

"Dare say," grunted Mrs. Biggs, and departed dangling the socks from her fingertips. Mr. Mather looked at the window and said in faintly surprised tones: "Do they know you've come out in this?"

"Yes. Well, no. Well, they do now."

"Shouldn't I telephone and tell them where you are?"

"Oh, don't bother," said Polly; then remembered

what her aunt had said last time. "At least . . . well . . ."

"Right."

The telephone was on the desk, and Polly listened hard to Mr. Mather's side of the conversation and tried to work out whether the crackle that was Aunt Sylvia sounded cross or not.

". . . I just thought I'd better let you know that I have your niece Polly here . . . yes . . . oh no, no, I assure you . . . well yes, she was rather; we're drying her off . . . no, really . . . look, if it doesn't stop soon I'll drive her back . . . no, no trouble at all. Goodbye."

"I'm being an awful nuisance," said Polly dismally.

"Nonsense, I'm very pleased to see you. I was finding it very difficult to concentrate, and you make a delightful interruption. I can tell you my good news—"

There was a knock and he broke off, looking suddenly shy. Mrs. Biggs came in with some cocoa.

"I didn't make any for you, sir."

"No, that's quite right, Mrs. Biggs."

When she had gone again he said: "Margaret's coming to stay tomorrow. I'm making the announcement this Sunday."

"Oh, I'm glad," said Polly.

Mr. Mather had already determined not to talk at great length about himself this time, and a silence fell while he pondered how to get Polly to say what was wrong. She seemed absorbed in scooping froth off her cocoa and eating it from the spoon.

"You look a little under the weather," he remarked finally. "In more senses than one. Sorry."

Polly turned luminous, haunted eyes on him. She

seemed not to notice his pun. "I'm . . . I . . . please don't laugh."

"I promise I won't."

"It sounds so silly. Look, do you believe in ghosts?"

After a moment he said: "I'm prepared to believe in yours."

"Mine? How did you—?"

"Am I right, then? You think you've seen one?"

"I haven't seen her," she said quickly. "But she haunts my room. She cries. I hear her."

"Good heavens, how very upsetting." He began to play with a pencil, hoping he didn't look as inadequate as he felt. "Did you say 'she'?"

"Yes. I know who she is—well, I'm sure it must be her. It's a girl who used to live in the house; it was her room. I dream about her nearly every night. I dream I'm her. I know all kinds of things that happened to her."

"Tell me."

"All of it? It would take a long time."

"Never mind, go on."

Polly related the five dreams in a slightly condensed form.

"You dreamed all this?"

"Yes. It is funny, isn't it? Dreams just aren't sensible like that usually. But Uncle Clement . . ." She told him what her uncle's reaction had been.

"Does he know you're still having the dreams?"

"I haven't bothered to tell him. He thinks I make things up. He thinks I made the crying up."

"I wonder why."

"Well, nobody else hears it," said Polly, and un-happily recounted the details.

"That's their good fortune. You must be particularly receptive."

"So you do believe it's really there?"

"Yes," he said slowly. He looked worried. "Yes, I don't think you imagine it. As for making it up, why should you?"

"Well," said Polly reluctantly, "I always have made things up. I tell the little ones stories. I invented a ghost in our house. But I always knew it was invented, and I thought they did, too. Uncle Clement can't see the difference between that and this."

"Awkward." He frowned.

"I daren't sleep in that room any more. But if I tell them about last night, they'll say nothing happened."

He twiddled his pencil to and fro. "Look, I don't believe they're entirely unreasonable. If you discuss it with them quietly and tell them everything you've told me, surely they'll let you sleep somewhere else."

"Do you think so?" said Polly hopefully. "I'll try."

"It's not pleasant to be haunted," he said seriously, "but I think you're lucky in your ghost. Sarah seems to have been a likeable person; I feel sorry for her."

"I certainly did when I heard the crying," said Polly in heartfelt tones. "Oh, you can't imagine—it was so dreadfully sad."

"I wonder what became of her."

Polly's face closed. "I don't think I want any more dreams."

"It's hard that you should have to suffer her trials all

over again. It's an extraordinary situation." He pondered for a moment. "But I can't help wondering what he'd been up to to get those muddy shoes."

"Uncle Simon?" Polly's own interest began to awaken. "Sarah was too miserable to care, and I haven't been thinking about it much. But I suppose it was rather odd."

"Tired himself out somehow, don't you think? And he seems to have a heart condition."

"Oh, is that it?"

"I'm only guessing. . . . Silly to go exhausting himself when he'd just been warned not to, presumably."

"Well, I think he seemed a bit fed up with the doctor. Maybe he didn't like being told not to do things."

"By the way, there's one small point I've just thought of: he did write tracts. Unless it's another Simon Stampenstone, which seems unlikely. I found one or two in this study when I came—pious Victorian stuff." He cast about him vaguely. "I can't remember where I put them; I'm sorry." The study was not at all tidy, and Polly regretfully conceded the difficulties in the way of a search, though she would very much have liked to see something connected with Sarah.

"It's a pity she wasn't born here," he said, "then she'd be in the parish records."

Mrs. Biggs knocked, and came in with Polly's socks. "Dry," she announced. "Do you want lunch at one as usual, sir?"

Polly realized that it was already twenty to, and saw that the rain had practically stopped.

"I must go," she said. "Thank you very much for being so helpful. I'll do what you suggested."

Mr. Mather said he was glad to have been of help and hoped he would see her again before she left the district. She donned socks, shoes and raincoat under Mrs. Biggs's waiting gaze, and was seen to the door.

She walked slowly home, careful not to shake up her headache. Everything smelt fresh after the rain, and she went over the recent conversation in her mind and considered various ways of asking if she could sleep somewhere else.

When she arrived she found the others halfway through lunch, and Aunt Sylvia dressed to go out and looking impatient.

"So you're back at last; now perhaps I can go. Your meal is keeping warm in the kitchen."

"Thank you. I'm sorry I'm late," said Polly. Her aunt didn't reply.

When Polly had finished eating they all went outside. The overflow was running strongly and Polly's idea of boats across the lake was found to work, using pieces of stick. They played with them until the rain returned and drove them inside.

Polly decided her uncle would be the best person to talk to, particularly since her aunt still seemed annoyed with her. She couldn't say anything while the young ones were around; but after she had tucked Hugh into bed she went into the dining room, where she knew Uncle Clement would be.

"I saw Mr. Mather today," she began.

"So your aunt was just telling me. Apparently you went out in pouring rain without informing her, and left Michael in a terrible state because of some nonsense you'd been telling him about people who used to live in this house. She had considerable difficulty calming him down. Don't you think it's unkind of you to upset him in this way?"

"I'd forgotten about that," said Polly guiltily. "Oh dear. Was he really very upset? He wanted to hear the story, you see; I've been telling it to them all along, but of course the last part was rather nasty. It upset me, too, when I dreamed it."

"Apparently Frederick mentioned something about it being based on dreams—the ones you told me about, I suppose."

"Yes, but I've had others since then. I have them every night."

"They're the effect of an overheated imagination, no doubt. Well, if you had to recount your nightmares, couldn't you at least have explained that that was all you were doing? Michael seemed to think you were telling them real events."

Polly took a breath and plunged. "I think I was. Mr. Mather thinks so too. He—he said I ought to tell you everything."

"He should know better than to encourage you," muttered her uncle. "Well, go on."

But having started off on the wrong foot Polly continued badly, stumbling over her tale so much that it didn't sound very credible even to herself. ". . . so please, could I sleep somewhere else?" she finished up.

"Sleep somewhere else?" echoed her aunt, coming in with the dinner.

"Polly thinks her room is haunted," said Uncle Clement grimly.

"It is." Polly felt desperate. "I can't spend another night there."

"Oh really, dear, don't you think you're carrying this a bit too far?"

"Mr. Mather believes me."

"Mr. Mather has no experience of children," said her uncle. "And where did he propose you should sleep instead?"

"This house isn't a hotel," said her aunt.

It somehow hadn't occurred to Polly that there were no free bedrooms. "I could go in with Jennifer," she pleaded after a moment.

"Do you really expect us to dismantle your bed at this time of night, carry it downstairs, wake your sister, and upset her by explaining why we're doing it?" asked her uncle reasonably.

"I could have a mattress on the floor. And I could easily invent a reason."

"Yes, I'm sure you could," said her uncle drily.

"You can't possibly sleep on the floor," said her aunt. "It's quite out of the question. Now please let's hear no more about it."

"I've just remembered something," said Polly frantically. "I've dreamed Mr. Stampenstone wrote tracts, and it's true; Mr. Mather's got some in his study."

"And no doubt you knew that before you dreamed it," said her uncle.

"No, I didn't! He only told me today!"

"Are you sure?"

Polly felt herself grow scarlet. She was too angry to speak, and bolted several mouthfuls of dinner instead.

Then she thought her blush had probably looked guilty; but it was too late to speak now. The food she had swallowed made her feel rather sick. She began to play with what remained on her plate.

"Don't you want that, Polly?" said her aunt after a while. "You haven't eaten very much, have you?"

The slight concern in her voice was Polly's undoing. "Don't feel hungry," she muttered with bowed head; but next moment two tears splashed into her gravy, making further concealment impossible.

"Good heavens, you don't look very well."

"I've got a headache," said Polly, mopping at the tears which, to her vexation, continued to flow.

"Have you had it long?"

"All day." Polly realized she was feeling dreadful. It was a comfort to have people bothering, but she wished she could stop crying.

"Come on." Uncle Clement appeared at her elbow. "Over to an armchair, that's right. Don't want any more dinner, do you? No. A couple of aspirins are what you need. You should have asked for something earlier."

She swallowed the aspirins when they arrived, and leaned back in the chair.

"And now straight to bed," said Uncle Clement, "and give them a chance to act. I'll help you up the stairs."

Polly agreed weakly, feeling stupid; but when they reached the door of her room she drew back, remembering.

"Come on now," said her uncle. "You're going to be asleep in a few minutes and you know there's nothing to be afraid of really. You're a big girl, remember. Do you want your aunt to help you undress?"

"No, thank you," said Polly mechanically, allowing him to steer her into the room.

"I'll come up in half an hour's time, but I know you'll be asleep. And when you wake up in the morning you'll be quite better. All right? Good night, then."

"Good night."

After he had gone Polly glanced round the room. Everything looked ordinary and safe; and the bed was cool and smooth. Very soon she was inside.

11 ✿ *The Middle of the Night*

She was Sarah again, and the time was the middle of the afternoon on the following day. She had been keeping herself too busy to brood, with the result that she had come to the end of her jobs early. Uncle Simon was in his study; he was back to normal today. The bare, tidy kitchen depressed her, and she knew her empty room would depress her even more. She decided to go outside.

Thugdon ran up as she closed the back door and she greeted him affectionately. He seemed to realize that she would play with him today, and bounded round her waving his tail and snapping his teeth in mock rage. She felt apologetic for having neglected him lately.

Her intended walk in the wood became a run, with Thugdon leaping tirelessly ahead. When he plunged into the middle of a patch of bluebells she called to him, laughing and breathless:

"Oh, Thugdon, get out of them, you clumsy great dog! You're crushing them!"

They were the first she had seen this year. Thugdon

trotted to her side while she tenderly rescued the snapped stems and sniffed their wild smell. He reached up to sniff them too, and knocked them from her hand with his eager nose.

"*Thugdon!*" She spoke severely this time. He rolled his eyes anxiously. "Hang your head!" she continued. "Go on! And your tail!"

When he looked suitably dejected she patted him.

Later they came to the point where the stream ran through the wall. Something had been going on here: a pile of damp sods lay on the bank, as though they might have been used recently to dam the hole. She suddenly wondered if this had been how Uncle Simon got his muddy shoes; and when she looked downstream and saw the rest of his activity, she knew.

"How . . . pretty," she said slowly. "Thugdon, imagine him building a pool!" It was impossible.

She gazed at the reflections until she had a childish desire to ruffle the mirror surface, and found a piece of stick. Thugdon gave a short eager bark and began to dance about.

"Oh, Thugdon, you fool, this isn't the lake!"

But he looked so disappointed that she threw it in for him all the same, leaping back to avoid the spray as he plunged after it. He caused such a commotion in the small pool that he lost the stick; and she was too busy watching his search to notice the figure slowly ascend the hill until a twig cracked not far away.

"Thugdon, come out," she said in a low, urgent voice. The dog didn't hear, but her uncle did; he jerked up his head and came hurrying towards them.

"Come out!" cried Sarah, and simultaneously:

"Here, sir!" bellowed her uncle.

Thugdon leaped out in a triumphant shower of drops; flicked a glance at his master and trotted up to lay the stick at Sarah's feet. She shrank from her uncle's expression and did not dare say a word to the dog.

"You—you—you!" He was too angry to speak coherently. "Prying—*interfering!*"

"I wasn't prying, sir—I was just . . . having a look—"

"And making my dog help you!" he roared. "As for him—here, sir, AT ONCE!"

Thugdon slunk across obediently. Uncle Simon grasped his walking-stick and the dog cowered, flattening himself towards the ground.

"I'll teach you to come when you're called," he said through gritted teeth. "I'll teach you whom you obey."

The heavy stick rose and fell. Thugdon howled.

"Oh no!" cried Sarah. "Don't! Don't beat him! It was my fault, not his!"

She stumbled forward, half blinded by tears. She heard another blow and another howl. Then she caught at her uncle's arm; she saw his face, purple and distorted with fury, and heard his wordless bellow; she saw the stick coming at her, and tried to dodge . . .

. . . and was knocked to the ground by the weight of her uncle's body.

The breath was crushed out of her. It was seconds before she could pull herself free. She scrambled up, bruised and shaken. Thugdon hadn't moved; and her uncle, unmoving too, lay where he had fallen.

"Sir . . ." she said timidly. "Are you all right? . . . Sir . . ." And presently: "Uncle . . . ?"

It was some time before she dared touch him. When she did she knew he was dead.

The nightmare had reached the ultimate point of horror. Polly woke.

Her relief lasted less than a second. Bewilderment replaced it. For a moment she thought she must still be sleeping. She wasn't in her room. She stood amid moonlit trees; a few yards away was the wall, and at her feet ran the stream.

How could she really be out here in the middle of the night, shivering in pajamas and bare feet? The moon was bright enough to show her that she was just next to the dam they had destroyed; and as she recoiled she knew with dread that this was no dream.

Yet after all, why be afraid? She knew the history of the pool now: who had made it, and how it had caused his death. It served him right. She was even gladder than before that they had destroyed it.

The stream ran shallow where the bed of the pool had been. It held her eyes, and stopped her running away.

There was something there, under the water. A shape that was too regular to be right. Like the corner of a trunk.

Suddenly she knew why the pool had been made. It was a hiding place. Uncle Simon had buried something underneath it . . . buried treasure . . . money?

She was just about to have a closer look when a nasty thought struck her. He had died just here, right where she was standing. Suppose Sarah's wasn't the only ghost? Suppose he still guarded his hoard?

The hairs on the back of her neck stood up. *There was someone behind her.*

She tried to run, tripped and fell headlong. A stone rushed up to meet her.

When Frederick woke to the sound of crying his first thought was one of cool astonishment. So it was true after all. A moment later he began to experience what he recognized as the physical symptoms of extreme fright. "This'll teach you to be skeptical," he thought; but not aloud, in case his voice should tremble.

The crying continued. Gathering courage from its faintness, he got out of bed and opened his door. Yes, it really did come from Polly's room.

Polly! She was up there, with—whatever it was. And she had been so frightened; and they had made her sleep there again.

"Come on," he thought sternly. "Polly went up when she heard it. You've got to do the same. Stop that shaking."

He edged slowly along the landing, then took the stairs at a run, flinging open the door and switching the light on all in one movement. A small solid figure stood by the bed, blinking and silenced.

"Were *you* making all that noise?" demanded Frederick.

"Yes," sniffed Hugh. "I can't find Number Three, and now Polly's gone as well."

The bed was empty.

"I suppose she's in the bathroom, you idiot." Reaction made him angry.

"She isn't, 'cos I went there myself."

Something made Frederick go over to the window and look out. He stiffened. Surely that was a movement among the trees. What on earth was going on?

"You go back to bed," he said with forced kindness. "I think Polly's—er—gone for a little stroll. I'll bring her back."

Hugh allowed himself to be persuaded. He couldn't have noticed that all Polly's clothes were still on the chair.

Frederick dressed rapidly, feeling anxious. He thought Polly might be sleepwalking, but he had never heard of a sleepwalker going so far. When he got outside there was no sign of her anywhere; he wondered if it could have been something else he had seen.

He went a little farther just to make sure, shining his torch around him, and then he found her. She was lying motionless by the broken dam, half in and half out of the stream, with her head next to a large boulder. He dragged her clear, and found a large bump on her temple; the skin was grazed, and bleeding slightly.

He spoke to her and splashed water on her face, which was one of the few parts that wasn't wet already. She didn't stir. Suddenly anxious, he felt for her pulse; but it was there all right. It was a good thing he had had first-aid lessons, he thought, and could manage a fireman's lift. He got her in position and began to stagger down through the wood.

He was exhausted when he reached the house and dumped Polly rather unceremoniously on the kitchen floor. After resting for a moment or two he went to wake his parents. Alarmed and incredulous, they came downstairs. Uncle Clement took one look at Polly and went to telephone a doctor; when he returned, she was opening her eyes. Her face was first confused and then frightened. "The money," she said.

"How do you feel, dear? Does anything hurt?" asked her aunt.

"My head," said Polly faintly, and closed her eyes again.

"We must get these wet clothes off her and put her to bed," said her uncle.

"No," said Polly.

"Don't worry, dear, they'll go away," said her aunt.

"No," repeated Polly.

Frederick was fairly sure it wasn't modesty that bothered her. After having mistaken Hugh for a ghost he could sympathize, albeit illogically, with her feelings on that subject. "It's the room," he said. "Put her in my bed. I don't mind."

"She's surely not still thinking of that. Is it that, Polly?"

"Yes." Her face relaxed.

"Well, I suppose she can go in your bed. Is your room tidy for when the doctor comes?"

"I'm going to pick you up now, Polly," said Uncle Clement. "Can you put your arms round my neck? Yes, that's good."

Polly frowned. "The money," she said.

"What money, dear?"

"In the pool."

They exchanged glances and asked no further questions.

When the doctor arrived she was tucked up in Frederick's room, clean and dry. "She seems very confused," they told him before he went in.

"Shock and slight concussion," he said afterwards. "I've given her something to make her sleep. I'll call again tomorrow."

Polly slept soundly, with shelves of medicines next to her head.

12 ♔ *Inside the Trunk*

"Have you been in to Polly yet?" asked Uncle Clement as he ate his breakfast next morning.

"No. It's early, I suppose she's still sleeping." Aunt Sylvia yawned. "I wish I was. What a night."

"It sounds callous of me, I guess, but it will be a great relief to me when that young lady goes home. Her fantasies will be her parents' responsibility then. I must say if I were they I'd think about taking her to a psychiatrist."

"What was it the doctor said?"

"He thought the anxiety over this haunting nonsense had probably precipitated the sleepwalking. She might have made for the pool because she'd been obsessed with that, too. But he'd never heard of anyone getting so far without hurting themselves before. It's a mercy Frederick saw her going and fetched her back so quickly. She might have lain there half the night."

"I wonder if she does it at home? John and Lucy might have warned us."

"With Lucy ill, I don't suppose they thought. Well, I must be off or I'll be late."

After he had gone Aunt Sylvia looked into Frederick's room. Polly stirred at once.

"What's happened to me?" she asked hoarsely. She was flushed and bright-eyed. "Why am I in here? What's wrong with my head? It's got a big lump on it."

"Don't try to sit up. How do you feel?"

"Horrible. What's happened?"

"You walked in your sleep last night. You went right out of the house, and Frederick found you up in the wood. You'd fallen and banged your head."

"In the wood?" Polly frowned, and then shuddered. "I remember now. I woke up, and I was by the pool. . . . Frederick found me?" She bounced up in the bed, but subsided again immediately, clutching her head with an agonized expression.

"Do lie still, dear, and try to keep covered up. You look as though you might have a chill, and no wonder, out there in nothing but pajamas and soaked to the skin."

"Did I fall into the pool?" She shuddered again. "How awful."

"Well, the pool isn't there any more, is it? But I gather you were where it used to be."

"Did Frederick say anything about a—a trunk?" she asked tensely.

"A trunk?" repeated Aunt Sylvia in surprise. "No, he didn't."

"Can he come in and see me?"

"He's not up yet."

"Can I see him as soon as he is?"

"Now calm down, you'll only make yourself feel worse. The doctor will be coming soon, and we'll have to see what he says about visitors."

"Visitors!" said Polly frantically. "But I'm not ill. My head hurts when I move it, that's all."

"You don't look at all well to me."

Aunt Sylvia was right; Polly had a chill. The doctor pronounced her temperature to be 101, and said she must stay in bed.

"She seems extremely anxious to see her cousin; she'll probably rest better if he's allowed to go in for a few minutes."

"I haven't called him yet, since he was up in the night."

"Yes, well there's no tremendous hurry."

The doctor departed, and the rest of the household came down to breakfast. Aunt Sylvia explained Polly's absence to the younger ones. "She's been asking to see you, Frederick; you can go up when you've finished eating."

"She never came and found Number Three," said Hugh.

"Why don't you listen? She was ill," snapped Frederick.

"I had to go to sleep without him," continued Hugh heavily. "I found him this morning, he was under my bed."

"Great," said Frederick sarcastically. He stood up. "I'll go and see Polly now."

Her eyes were closed and she looked very hot. Just as he was retreating she opened them and saw him.

"Fluff! Don't go away!"

"I'm sorry, did I wake you?"

"It doesn't matter. Fluff, Aunt Sylvia said you found me in the pool."

"Where the pool was," corrected Frederick.

Polly paid no attention. "You must have seen the chest. You did, didn't you?"

"Which chest?" asked Frederick carefully. Polly's eyes had a wild glitter that alarmed him.

"In the pool. The corner of it shows. Fluff, I've worked it all out; Uncle Simon buried his money there. He made the pool, you see; I dreamed it last night."

"But he hadn't any money," said Frederick, reluctantly humoring her. "He told that doctor so."

"That was just what he said, because he knew he might die and he didn't want Sarah to get it. So he hid it, and then he did die; it was in my dream. Then I woke up by the pool and I saw the corner of the chest under the water. Oh, Fluff, you must have seen it too!"

"Look, Polly." He rubbed his nose uncomfortably. "You mustn't start getting all upset. Your temperature—"

She grabbed his wrist. "I'm not upset; you must tell me, I shall be upset if you don't. Did you see it?"

"No, I didn't, because there's nothing there," he said firmly. "You were still asleep when you thought you saw it. It's quite natural; the blow on your head's confused you. If I were you I'd stop thinking about your nightmare and try to get some sleep." He disengaged his hand, and saw that tears were running down her cheeks.

"Are you feeling very bad? Shall I get Mother?"

"No. Fluff, will you go and *see?* Please say you will. I know it's there."

"Oh, Polly. . . ." What was the use of talking to her while she was in this state? "All right, I will." Here was an excuse to leave.

It sounded as though the younger ones were in the boys' room. As he went past his own name caught his ears.

". . . won't give Frederick any of my candy," said Hugh.

"You mean little boy," said Jennifer.

"He never has any of his own," said Michael.

"He could if he wanted to," replied Hugh, unmoved.

"He couldn't. You know Polly said he doesn't get any spending money."

"Yes, but it isn't true. I saw Uncle giving him three fifty-cent pieces on Friday."

"A dollar and a half!" Jennifer sounded completely disillusioned.

"Maybe it was a present," said Michael doubtfully.

"It was spending money. He said so."

Frederick found to his irritation that he was blushing. Really, wherever did Polly get her ideas? He didn't know whether to be touched or annoyed by her efforts on his behalf. He went on downstairs and his mother called from the dining room:

"Frederick, is that you?"

He dodged through the kitchen and out of the back door pretending not to have heard. He was sure she would be wanting him to amuse his cousins, and he felt more like avoiding them for the time being.

He found himself walking up the hill. He supposed he might as well go and look for Polly's chest. After all, she had meant well about the candy.

Of course there was nothing there. He had known there wouldn't be. Polly had been mistaken; easy enough, by moonlight. He picked up a stick and stirred the water into cloudy confusion. Who'd bury anything here, for heaven's sake?

The stick struck something hard. A stone? He bent down and felt in the mud with his fingers. It did feel remarkably like— He knelt, and was able to use both hands. Now he could see it: undoubtedly the corner of a box, or trunk.

He was glad there was nobody to witness his expression as he digested the fact. He soon worked out what had happened; the removal of the dam, together with the previous day's heavy rain, had exposed the buried object; then it must have got lightly covered again in the confusion of rescuing Polly from the water.

"Polly was right all the time," he said slowly. He jumped to his feet. Bare hands were no use here; he needed tools.

Polly, dozing uneasily, had lost all sense of time. The bed had become a checkerboard and she was the checkers, waging a ridiculous and interminable war on each other across the squares.

Michael rescued her, appearing beside the bed with an anxious face.

"Did I wake you?"

"I'm glad you did. I was twenty-four checkers."

"Oh . . . are you very ill?"

"No. Has Frederick been to look for the money?" she asked suddenly.

"I don't know. What money?"

"The money in the pool. Will you go and look, Michael?"

She heard her aunt's voice break in. "So there you are. Come away now, Polly isn't well enough to talk to you."

She wanted to protest, but found she had no energy.

"She's been saying such funny things," came Michael's fading voice.

"It's nothing, it's because she's feverish." The door closed.

"Frederick wasn't in with Polly," said Michael, rejoining the others in the drawing room.

"Aunt Sylvia's angry with him for vanishing," observed Jennifer, picking moodily at a scab on her knee. "Oh, why doesn't Polly get better? I'm so bored and there's nothing to do."

"She's feverish," said Michael gravely. "She said she was twenty-four checkers, and she's forgotten that we took the dam away."

"Why?" asked Hugh.

"Because she told me to go and look for some money in the pool." He wondered if he ought to tell Hugh to take his feet off the seat of the armchair.

Hugh stared vacantly; then said: "I mean why has she forgotten?"

"Because she's ill."

"Is there really some money there?" said Jennifer with interest.

"Oh no, I don't think so."

"Let's go and see." She went purposefully to the door.

"But—oh well, all right," said Michael, following her.

"I don't forget things when *I'm* ill," said Hugh to the air. "Come on, Number Three. We'd better go, too."

They passed Aunt Sylvia. "Are you going in the garden? Try to keep out of mischief, won't you. I expect you'll find Frederick somewhere."

They found him with his shoes and socks off, standing in the stream and struggling with a large muddy oblong.

"Look," said Hugh, in tones of deep pleasure. "Mischief."

Frederick's room was full of people. It was almost like a party, thought Polly as she sat up in bed and recounted her last dream to an audience so large it made her shy. Not only were her uncle and aunt there, but Mr. Mather and "my fiancée, Margaret Jameson" as well.

Polly's temperature was down to normal. She had slept soundly all afternoon, secure in the knowledge that the precious chest stood outside the back door (Aunt Sylvia refused to have it in the house until it had dried off) and wouldn't be touched until Uncle Clement got home. ("I think I could break the lock," Frederick had said, "but Mother won't let me try. Anyway, you must be there when it's opened, Polly.")

Then she had awakened, feeling much better; and had eaten soup and pudding while people popped in and out to see how she was and bring messages.

"Mr. Mather called, he's coming and bringing a lady. He wants to tell you something."

"Uncle Clement's home, we're just going to show him the chest."

"They're going to bring the chest up here."

It was standing on sheets of newspaper in the corner, a squat black metal trunk. Polly glanced at it continually to reassure herself that it was real.

". . . he was dead," she concluded at last.

"What did he die of?" asked Hugh.

"What happened to Sarah then?" asked Michael.

"I don't know," said Polly. "I woke up then." She had already admitted the source of the story to the younger ones.

"I think I can tell you the rest," interposed Mr. Mather.

"Can you?" exclaimed Polly. "But how?"

"Thanks to an inspiration of Margaret's." He smiled at her and she blushed faintly. "She asked me if there were any of Mrs. Piper's descendants still living in the parish. We had a look in the records and found a Mrs. Woodstock whose maiden name was Piper. . . ."

"Old Mrs. Woodstock?" said Uncle Clement. "She has the cottage with the fine garden, hasn't she?"

"That's right. We called on her, and found we were in luck: her mother used to work for Simon Stampenstone."

"And Sarah—does she remember Sarah?" begged Polly.

"She remembers his niece coming to live with him, though at first she'd forgotten the name. She was only a child herself at the time, but she used to hear her mother talk about it. And his death made a big impression on her because it was so dramatic—a heart attack brought on by losing his temper with the dog, they said. It was very upsetting for Sarah; apparently she scarcely spoke a word for a whole day afterwards. Mrs. Piper came up here and stayed with her while they made arrangements, and after the funeral she went to live with her former schoolteacher."

"Miss Swirles," said Polly with satisfaction; and added: "So that proves it, doesn't it? She was really real."

"Yes, Polly," said Uncle Clement heavily. "We owe you an apology."

Embarrassed, she muttered something inaudible and changed the subject quickly. "Did he leave her any money?"

"He left no will and no money. Everyone was rather surprised; he had a reputation for meanness, and they thought there'd be a good bit tucked away. But I believe that's what you think you've found?" He glanced at the children's eager faces, and Polly nodded vigorously.

"He certainly sounds a likely miser," he mused. "That might have been why he had Thugdon—to guard his hoard."

Uncle Clement coughed. "I think we're straying into the realms of fancy there."

"It seems to be a point we could check," said the minister mildly, eyeing the trunk.

"Yes, Dad. Do open it now," urged Frederick.

"Well, perhaps this is the moment." He knelt down

and delved into his tool bag; they moved back a little to give him room to work. "We mustn't be too hopeful," he cautioned. "It may very well be empty."

"Who would bury an empty trunk?" said Polly. "I know it's the money, I know it is."

"If he didn't want his niece to have it, why couldn't he make a will leaving it to someone else?" asked Aunt Sylvia, whose tone of polite interest contrasted strongly with the suppressed excitement of Uncle Clement's.

"Perhaps because there wasn't anyone else," said Mr. Mather slowly. "Sarah was his only living relative, and he doesn't seem to have had any close friends. If he was a real miser he'd be a little mad on the subject; unable to bear the idea of anyone having his precious money—and of course Sarah would have inherited it automatically if he died without leaving a will."

"Ah ha," said Uncle Clement to himself, "beginning to get somewhere." He added more loudly, "If by any chance it should be money, I shall certainly see that you children each get a prize for finding it."

Under cover of the younger ones' delighted babble Polly whispered to Mr. Mather: "But it isn't his."

Margaret gave her a quick smile. "I feel rather like that, too," she murmured.

"But it isn't, is it?"

"You know, I think it is," whispered the minister. "It was found on his land, you see."

"But it's Sarah's." Tears of indignation stood in her eyes. Luckily the others were crowding round Uncle Clement, with their backs turned and no attention to spare for her.

"It was once," agreed Mr. Mather. "But don't you think Sarah is quite possibly dead by now?"

"I know she is," said Polly, diverted. "Or she couldn't haunt me."

Margaret spoke into the minister's ear. "The letter."

"I'd forgotten." He felt in his pocket. "Here, Polly. Mrs. Woodstock let us have it; I thought you'd like it. A letter from Sarah to Mrs. Piper. . . ."

"It's opening!" cried several voices.

"Let me see!" exclaimed Polly, craning from the bed.

Slowly the lid creaked up, and the contents of the trunk were revealed. It was half filled by a mass of jumbled gray-brown fragments rather like dead leaves; except that some still had corners, and on some ghostly figures still showed.

There was an awful silence. Uncle Clement made the quickest recovery. "The fool buried bills," he said conversationally, as though he had guessed it all along, "and the damp got in." He touched a fragment bearing the legend $20. It crumbled into tiny pieces.

Frederick was the next to find a voice.

"What a waste!" he groaned. "All that money!"

"Dust and ashes," said Mr. Mather softly. "To think it once killed a man. If he hadn't worn himself out making the pool he probably wouldn't have had a fatal attack next day."

"I wonder how much there was?" Jennifer pondered.

"Oh well," said Frederick, striving to be philosophical, "it rounds off the story. And you guessed right." He gave Polly a small grin.

"Yes, it's nice to know." She sniffed the faint musty smell that hung in the air. "Dead money. What can we do with it?"

"Throw the lot away," said Uncle Clement shortly. "It's worthless." He gathered up his tools and went out.

"Dirty stuff," said Aunt Sylvia distastefully, closing the lid. "Now it's bedtime for you younger ones, and Polly must get some sleep after all the excitement. Can we offer you some sherry before you go?"

"That's very kind of you." Mr. Mather lingered for a moment while Aunt Sylvia shooed the others out. "Disappointed?" he murmured.

"I . . . don't know," said Polly slowly.

"The money meant an awful lot to him," he said, "but the lack of it couldn't really hurt Sarah. She escaped; that was all she cared about."

"I wonder why her ghost is a child?" mused Polly, who found she could talk about it quite easily now.

"I think there never was an actual, palpable (if that doesn't sound too much a contradiction in terms) ghost. You were haunted by her unhappiness, you could say."

"But I won't be any more," said Polly with certainty.

"No. Well, goodbye, Polly. I hope I see you again before you go."

"Goodbye, and thank you very much for the letter."

When he had gone she drew it out and looked at it. The ink had faded, but Sarah's sloping, curly hand was still clear.

My dear Mrs. Piper,
I thought maybe you would like to know that

Gray One has settled down very well here. Thank you again very much for keeping him for me, and I'm sorry I took him away again so soon except I'm sure he was a nuisance to you really. And thank you for looking after me so kindly until Miss Swirles could come for me.

It is so lovely to be back in a place I know. Miss Swirles says she was worried about me all the time; she wrote again (after Uncle Simon made me send the horrid letter) but as I never got it I think he must have been watching the mail in case, and burnt it.

I am going to be a teacher at her school. I can't really believe it; it is so exactly what I would like to do. In two years' time I can begin with the little ones, and I'm going on learning until then. It's funny but I'm so pleased to be doing lessons again. I thought she had told Uncle Simon I was stupid but she only said I was "not brilliant, but a good steady worker."

Everyone in the school likes Gray One. When I start teaching he will be a help; don't you think they will learn "the cat sat on the mat" much more quickly if they can see a real cat doing it in the classroom?

Thank you again, for everything. I am so happy.

Yours affectionately,
Sarah.